ON TWO FEET

AND FOUR PAWS

BY

GIULIANA GIUSTI CHINES

For Paolo,

Giulia, Emma and Beatrice,

who brighten my life

Translated by Giuliana Giusti Chines

Original title: *Su Due Piedi e Quattro Zampe*.

ISBN | 978-88-91148-65-0

Many thanks to my former colleague and dear friend Manuela Pucci for reading this book and correcting the mistakes, and to my new friend Lisa Clifford for her scrupulous editing, for her encouragement and the helpful suggestions she offered.

Many thanks also to Astrid Lucchesi for her beautiful illustrations, which add so much value to the book.

CONTENTS

CHAPTER ONE

(Thursday, 14th July)

Who's the leader?

My name is Teo Teodorico Thedog Stupidbeast Sillydog.

Tommy is my best friend. His other names are Tommaso Lazybones Sleepyhead.

Tommy's Mum and Dad are called Mum Marianna Painintheneck and Dad Corrado Misterno.

As I have the longest name, I feel I should be considered the leader of this pack, but no-one seems to recognize my authority. Actually, I'm ordered about all the time and I'm not even allowed to sleep in the house. I live in the garden and I sleep on the grass. There's a small shelter I get in when it rains or it's too cold, but I generally stay out in the open, day and night.

In the evening I go to the window and Marianna gives me a biscuit. It's evening now and I'm waiting. I've been waiting with my nose stuck to the glass for a while already, but Marianna is not in sight. I can only see the sofa with the back of Corrado's head sticking out and the animated pictures in the television in front of him.

There's no trace of Tommy. He must be in the other room, playing with THE COMPUTER.

Why isn't Marianna coming? She must have forgotten I'm waiting for the biscuit.

Oh, I was wrong, after all! Here she comes at last! See? I tend to be too pessimistic, sometimes...

"Go... go... goooo! Good goooo!"

Oh, my gosh! Marianna has stopped midway because of that horrible howl coming from the other room. "Go to bed, Tommaso!" she yells. "Do it NOW!!! Enough of that COMPUTER!"

"Five more minutes, please..." Tommy says.

Misterno jumps up from the sofa and bellows: "Obey without arguing!"

"Just one more minute... I'm about to break my record!" Tommy implores

"OBEY WITHOUT ARGUING, I said!"

Silence.

Now Tommy comes into sight. He's shuffling his feet and staring at the ground. When he shuffles his feet and stares at the ground I know he feels miserable.

"It's so early!" he complains. "And I don't have to go to school tomorrow morning."

"Not to school, of course, but you have SOCCER PRACTICE, don't you?"

Tommy hates the words SOCCER PRACTICE. Every time someone says these words his spirits flunk. Besides Corrado has a very stern face now. When he has such a stern face, Tommy knows he's not someone to cross. So he just gives a little kick to the leg of the table and drags himself upstairs.

I sigh with affliction because I won't see him again until tomorrow morning. Anyway, at this point, Marianna should give me the biscuit. Is it my impression or she's definitely getting nearer? Yes! She's coming! Hurray! I lick my lips, whimper and wag my tail frantically.

Now she's stopped behind the window and she's scowling at me. Good gosh! Why is she scowling? What did I do wrong? And where's THE BISCUIT? I can't see ANY BISCUIT!!! Isn't there A BISCUIT?

Instead of giving me THE BISCUIT, Marianna screams: "Go away, stupid beast, you're smearing the glass with your clammy nose!"

No biscuit tonight.

I'll go, then. What else can I do?

I put my sagging tail between my legs and I slowly set off for the lawn. I go to the jasmine bush, which is my favourite spot for sleeping. Here I take a deep sigh, turn round a couple of times to make my bed and then I lie down. The moon is so big tonight it almost sits on my head. It looks like an inflated balloon and it floodlights the sky hiding the stars. I close my eyes and I might very well go to sleep, but then I remember I haven't sung to the moon yet. I can't fall asleep if I don't sing to the moon first. So I sit up, yawn, scratch behind the ear, raise my face to the sky and start singing.

Oh, moooooooooooooooon.....
you're a beaming ballooooooon ....
don't go away toooo soooooooon ...
I love you dear mooooooon.....

Landing On The Mattress

Is

that the coach over there

waving at me

from the middle

of the football ground?

I wave back,

then I suddenly see

there's someone else behind him.

Two people, it seems.

They' re far away, though...

just two speckles in the background

but moving fast ahead

and getting bigger by the second...

Oh, no! I know who they are!

Run! I say to myself,

but I can't move an inch.

My legs are stuck to the ground

and all of a sudden,

one of the blokes covers the distance

with a big jump

and springs up in front of me.

There's a horrible sneer

on his revolting face,

which is full of piercings and pimples.

The other nerd is right at my back now

and he's tailing me so closely

I can feel his putrid breath

on my neck.

I'm lost!!!

A huge claw clutches my shoulder

and a horrible pain gripes my stomach.

I cry out loud

and I dart forward at last,

but I lose hold of the ground

and I start falling.

And I fall and fall...

and my head gets faint,

and my stomach jumps up to my throat.

I shout again and I keep shouting

as I keep falling until...

until I land on the mattress, my heart hammering so hard that I feel as if it's going to jump out of my chest...

What a heck! That sickly nightmare again!

And Teo howling like mad!

It's lucky he woke me up, though. There's no way to say how long the nightmare would have lasted if he hadn't. The only problem is I won't be able to go back to sleep now. How can I possibly sleep with Teo making that racket? And the sickly question sticking at the back of my mind: WHERE CAN I FIND THE MONEY?

There's clear evidence that mum has started to be suspicious. The other day she opened and closed her wallet three times and then she asked Dad if, by any chance, He'd taken HER money. Dad hit the roof and yelled that HE had nothing to do with HER PRECIOUS MONEY and that SHE ought to take CARE of HER OWN THINGS!

Actually, this is true. Mum has become very absent-minded lately. She keeps losing everything: her cellphone, her glasses, her keys, the shopping list, her jacket, her handbag... Last week she even lost a shoe!

She also forgets to do things. That's why she bought a small notepad to write what she's supposed to remember in it. Unfortunately, she lost her notepad, too.

Anyway, I can't go on taking her money forever. I've already done it three times... twenty Euros each time. She's sure to catch me sooner or later. But there's no way out I'm afraid.

If only I could never go to that damn soccer practice again! Also because I'm such a poor player and the coach never lets me play at matches. I just sit on the bench like a perfect idiot and watch the others play.

Unfortunately, I've already tried all possible excuses for not going: headaches, sore-throats, a sprained ankle, tooth-aches, coughing fits, stomach-aches, cramps, hiccups. None of them worked and I don't know what else I might think of.

The problem is Dad has set his mind on making me play soccer. He says he doesn't want me to loaf about all day... "Especially now that there are no schoolmates you can play with. Haven't they all gone to the seaside?" he says.

True. All my best friends seem to have vanished into thin air. They may not all have gone to the seaside, but when I call them on the phone they never seem to be there...

I wouldn't mind staying on my own though, if I could have one of the latest games... Creepers, or Mummification would be perfect. Even The Secret Mountain would be OK, even though it isn't so gory as the others.

But Dad doesn't want me to buy new video-games. "You already have far too many of them!" he says. "Can't you see video-games eat your brain, the little of it that is left?" he also says.

Unfortunately, he also thinks I have a really good time playing soccer and he's convinced that I'm a sort of budding champion.

It was me who put this idea in his head.

That's because he kept asking: "How many goals did you score today?" and I once lost my patience and told him I'd scored three goals and that the coach had said I showed promise. Unfortunately, Dad believed me...

What time is it now? Still eleven o'clock? Luckily Teo is no longer howling. Everything is so quiet now... but I can't go back to sleep all the same. The fact is I know what my real problem is. It's not soccer, really.   I wish I could tell someone about it, but I can't. No way!

What's the time now? I can't believe it! Is it still eleven, one minute and fifteen seconds? Time's stuck tonight.

A delicious Smell
of Rotten Fish

I''ve

smelled it!

It can't be too far...

There it is!

Wow! It's a squirrel!

20

How big!

Oh, heck! It's gone!

Where is it?

Where has it gone?

Humph, I've lost it!

But what's this other smell?

this delicious smell of....

rotten fish?

Rotten fish?

If it's rotten fish it must be Bigongio!

I'm happy he's coming! He hasn't shown up for some time.

I'd be tempted to fly at him at once, but I don't want to spoil the game. Better stay still and pretend I haven't seen him. I shut one eye and squint at him with the other.

The silly cat is padding on in front of me in his soft velvet sneakers now, his bulky backside swaying next to my nose.

I think it's time for me to do my part now.

Ready?

FORWARD!!!

I jump up and I start barking at the top of my voice.

Bigongio turns into a huge ball of fur. Quite frightening, I admit, but I don't budge an inch and keep barking furiously.

At last Bigongio runs away. High time he did!

He runs like a shot and I chase him. He climbs up the fig tree, gets to the top and sits on a branch. I sit under the tree and Bigongio starts cleaning himself. I think he's trying to gain time... but he should know it's no use. I won't stir from here.

I have to wait a bit, but at last Bigongio starts

meowing and I start singing my song.

Mine and Bigongio's voices blend in the air breaking the silence of the night like blaring sirens.

In no time the house lights turn on and Corrado's grim face appears at the window, his hair standing on end.

"STOP IT!" he bellows, joining the choir.

"STOP IT, both of you, stupid beasts!

GET AWAY, you silly dog! GET LOST!

Did you HEAR what I SAID?

GET AWAY or the stupid cat won't GET DOWN the tree!

"GET AWAY IMMEDIATELY, I said!"

I don't budge an inch and I go on singing at the top of my voice, while Bigongio goes on meowing as if he was being flayed alive.

After a while, Corrado opens the front door and strides towards me, his pyjamas half unbuttoned, his slippers shuffling on the wet grass and a threatening look in his eyes. Then he grabs my collar and drags me towards home and into the house, down the hall and up to the cupboard under the staircase. After that, he shuts me up in the cupboard.

HERE I AM AT LAST! This is just WHERE I WANT TO BE! There are such DELICIOUS SMELLS here, with all those salami, hams and sausages dangling from the ceiling! They're out of reach like Bigongio up on the fig tree but, at least, I can SNIFF them!

After a while, I get tired of just sniffing and having nothing to eat, though, so I decide to hit the sack. I find myself a good place between the broom and the bucket, I turn round a couple of times and I lie down with a big sigh.

Up there, on the fig tree, Bigongio is still launching his appalling shrieks to the sky. I'm so happy I can't resist the temptation to join him again, even though the moon can't be seen from here.

Oh, moooooooooooooooon....

you're a beaming ball...

"Shut up, silly dog!"

Oh, heck! They heard me!

Also Dogs Snore

Did

I hear Teo howl again? He must be in the

cupboard now.

Poor chap! He must be desperate.

That awful cat keeps coming into the garden and

Teo gets mad. They make such an appalling racket together that Dad has to get out of bed and put Teo in.

The problem is he shuts him in that smelly cupboard. Poor Teo! He must be chocking in that stuffy hole! I can't leave him there! I know what I'll do. I'll go fetch him! I only have to be sure Mum and Dad have fallen asleep again.

What time is it? It's one, eight minutes and two seconds. Time to go.

I toss my blanket aside and get up. The bed squeaks and I catch by breath. Luckily nobody seems to have heard. I walk to the door barefoot. It's ajar and I push it open. I grope my way across the landing, then I quietly step down the stairs. I haven't switched on any of the lights, but my eyes are quickly getting used to the darkness and I can make out the outline of the furniture in the hall now. Teo must have heard me as he's whimpering and thumping his tail.

I open the cupboard door. Before I can see him, Teo jumps up, puts his legs on my shoulders and starts licking my face, his tail thumping against the bucket. "Be quiet, good boy." I whisper patting his head. "Calm down or they'll hear us."

Teo sits down.

"You're the brightest dog in the world." I whisper again, kissing him on the nose. Teo breathes heavily and gives me his paw.

"Shush! Don't make all that noise! Let's go. "

I head for the stairs and Teo follows me.

We sneak past Mum and Dad's bedroom and there we are! Just the time to shut the door and we both rush for the bed. I slip under the blankets and Teo settles on my feet. In a matter of minutes he starts snoring. Also dogs snore... I didn't know.

CHAPTER TWO

(Friday, 15th July)

All Clear!

Whats

this shuffling and rattling? What's this clanking?

Where's this delicious smell coming from?

"Breakfast's ready!"

I open my eyes wide. Oh... good gosh! I'm in the

house and in the MOST FORBIDDEN PLACE in the world!

This is Tommy's bed!

WHAT SHALL I DO NOW?

What's Tommy doing?

He's lying face down, his head under the pillow.

IS HE SLEEPING?

I can't believe it!

What happens if they FIND ME HERE?

I must wake him up!

IMMEDIATELY!

I crawl on the bed until I get near Tommy's head. I thrust my head under the pillow and start licking his cheek. Tommy makes a face. The pillow falls onto the ground. I lick Tommy's cheek again.

Finally Tommy stirs, but he doesn't open his eyes. "Five more minutes…" he mumbles.

I give him some more big licks and he finally squints up at me. He stays still for a moment and then, all of a sudden, he jumps up and I jump backward.

"What time is it?" he asks, staring at me with wide open eyes.

I wag my tail. I don't know what the time is but

Mum and Dad are awake and I shouldn't be here!

"Tommy wake up! Breakfast's ready!" Marianna shouts again.

"Coming!" Tommy shouts back.

Then he whispers: "I'll put you out before someone sees you."

I keep wagging my tail. I'd like him to remember that I'm not supposed to be OUT but INSIDE! INSIDE THE CUPBOARD, actually!

"Don't make any noise." Tommy orders.

He puts on his slippers, then he thinks better of it and takes them off. After that, he walks across the room in his bare feet, holding the slippers in his hand. He signals to me to keep silent and stay behind as he opens the door trying not to make any noise. Then he puts his head out to see if there's anyone in sight. "All clear." he says under his voice. Then he starts padding down the stairs.

I go after him, ready to take to my heels in case either Marianna or Corrado turns up.

Now we've reached the bottom of the stairs... now we're walking across the hall...

"WHAT'S GOING ON HERE?"

I jump at the sound of Corrado's voice and hide behind Tommy's back. I can feel Tommy's scared stiff now.

"Nothing at all." he says jutting out his chin. "I just heard Teo call from the cupboard... I think he needs to go out."

"Hmm..." Corrado sets his jaw as he looks at Tommy's bare feet. "Get a move on!" he then says in a clipped voice. "You know you've got SOCCER PRACTICE this morning."

"Right." Tommy pulls a face and stares at the ground shifting from one foot to the other.

"Come on, then! Put the dog out before it gets dark again." Corrado barks.

Tommy and I jump to the door and half a second later I'm out.

Phew! Lucky escape this time!

The sun is high already and it makes the dewy grass shimmer.

Buried Bones

Here

I am, all alone in the scorching sun. Bees and bluebottles hum all around and flies come and sit on my nose. They're such a nuisance! But I'm so tired I don't have the strength to chase them.

Butterflies are flitting among the flowers. There's a lizard, too. It's baking in the sun next to my nose... Should

I try and catch it? I don't think so. That would be
exhausting...

There's a couple of little birds, too. They're sitting on
the grass and pecking away. I know a mere blink would
send them flying, but I don't care. They can stay as long
as they wish.

Unfortunately, the sun is scorching my back,
though. Sooner or later I'll have to find myself a nice,
shadowy place where I can sleep in peace. But is it worth
the effort?

I decide to resist. The sun will have to move away
sooner or later...

On second thoughts... I'm not so sure it's a good
idea to get scorched to the bones. Better look for a
shadowy spot somewhere.

I slowly pull myself up, shake off the flies, yawn,
stretch out my front legs, stretch out my hind legs, yawn
again, scratch behind the ear, lick my tummy and then I

drag myself to the fence.

I slump to the ground.

It was worth the effort, I must say. Here the shadow is deep and the air is light. A gentle wind is moving about.

Unfortunately, though, this windy air carries a faint smell of roast-beef with it and this suddenly reminds me of the treasure.

There are a lot of buried bones on the other side of the fence... a REAL TREASURE they are!

The burial spot can be clearly seen because of the uneven ground...

Those are Birillo's bones, unfortunately.

BIRILLO!!!

The SELFISH KNAVE!

THE MONGREL!

HOW UNFAIR! Why should he get ALL THOSE BONES while I have NONE?

He doesn't even look like a real dog, with that ridiculous red ribbon on his head and the sickly smell of shampoo sticking to his fur.

But he's wealthy, lucky him! His treasure of bones must be one of the biggest in the world.

He gets a brand-new bone every time our neighbour cooks the meat on the barbecue and, when this happens, he comes to the fence with the bone in his mouth to show off to me. When he's sure I've seen him, he sits down and starts gnawing.

At this point, my bowels turn upside-down and I lose my head. So I start barking, whimpering, whining, howling, growling, scampering up and down the fence, jumping up, clamping my teeth shut on the wire and shaking it violently...

I no longer know what I am doing but there's nothing I wouldn't do to get at one of those bones...

Unfortunately, there's nothing I can actually do.

I can't make holes in the damn fence and the MONGREL neither listens to my pleas nor minds my threats...

In the end, my tail and ears flop and I just sit still peering into the void.

At this point, the stinking mongrel buries the bone.

To do that, he digs a shallow hole in the ground and puts the bone in it, then he turns round and kicks some dirt in the air with his hind legs. After that, he goes away without even turning to see if the bone has been properly buried.

As soon as he's gone, I spring to my feet and, as a last resort, I start digging holes on my side of the fence. I dig plenty of very deep holes in no time. My purpose is that of opening a tunnel underground, which will hopefully take me to the other side.

But THIS NEVER HAPPENS and EVERY TIME Corrado GOES CRAZY.

The last time he caught me red pawed, he started bawling: "I've had enough of your stupid holes, you stupid beast!"

Our neighbour turned up on the other side of the fence and Corrado said: "Hi! How are you! This dog is a real calamity! I don't understand why he makes all these holes."

"I think he smells the barbecue" our neighbour said, "and he would like to get a bone. What if I give him one?"

I sprang up, my mouth open, my tail frenziedly wagging. What did she say? Did I get it right? Does she want to GIVE ME A BONE?

"No, thank you. The vet said bones are not good for dogs."

WHAT? I span round to stare at Painintheneck, who had suddenly appeared at my back.

"Aren't they?" our neighbour said. "Can't dogs eat bones? Never heard of that before!"

I span round to smile at our neighbour, then I span round again to look at Painintheneck with pleading eyes. SEE? ALL DOGS EAT BONES! Everybody KNOWS that!

But Painintheneck declared: "That's what I was told by the vet, so I'd rather my dog didn't get started on the habit. Sorry! See you." Then she turned on her heels and went inside.

Our neighbour shook her head and then she went away, too.

Corrado went back into the house and I was left alone.

I'd never felt so down in the dumps in my whole life before.

Icy Water

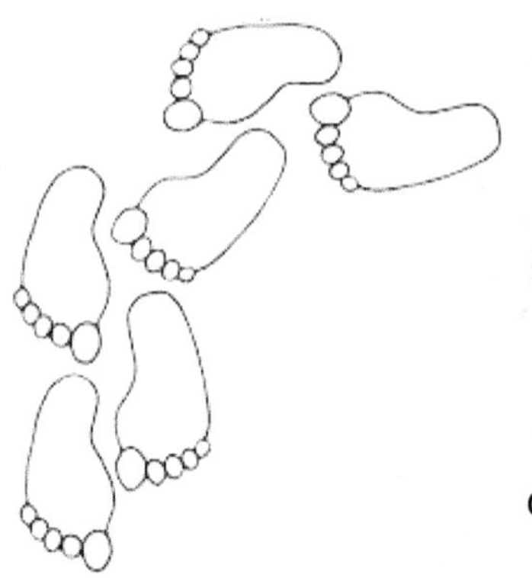

I didn't get the money.

I looked for mum's purse but it was nowhere to be found. Now I'm chasing the ball, up and down the football ground, with no result.

My mind is elsewhere. The problem is I've already seen The Two. They were striding along the lane, talking to each other, all their piercings and pimples in place, plus a brand new reddish crest sticking up on the top of the short nerd's head.

"Fweeeeeet!!!"

The coach must be whistling at me, I think. He must have noticed I'm a little out of sorts. The other day I managed to steal away before time off and it worked. The two blokes didn't expect me to leave before time and couldn't catch up to me. I think I'll do the same today. I might be lucky again.

I start chasing Marchesini, who's dribbling the ball, and when I reach him, I give him a good push, knocking him over. I hope the coach will call me out now.

"Tommaso Aladino, come here!" the coach yells.

PERFECT!

I get out of the playing area walking slowly, my head down and a grimace on my face. I want the coach to think I'm not feeling well.

"What's the matter with you Tommy Aladino, once and for all?" the coach croaks as soon as I appear in front of him. He's mad at me, I can see that. GOOD!

"Nothing." I say.

"Nothing, you said? Why then do you look as if you've just fallen out of bed, eh?"

The coach is furious now. VERY GOOD! Time for a nice little story.

"You see... it's... it's this awful... headache..." I stutter, staring at the ground and shifting from one foot to the other.

"A headache, eh?"

To my surprise the coach spreads his big hand on my brow. "You haven't got a temperature." he decrees. Then he rummages in his pocket and takes out a key. "Go into the changing rooms, take a shower and get dressed." he says, handing me the key. "But wait for us there, eh?"

I nod, trying not to show how happy I am.

"Got it? Don't steal away before time as you did the other day, eh?"

I nod again and I head towards the lane that takes to the changing rooms, trying not to walk too fast.

The coach said I must wait but I won't. I won't even have a shower. I'll just grab my bag and take to my heels at once.

I've been trying not to show I'm hurrying in case the coach is looking at me, but when I know I can no longer be seen from the football ground, I spring up and run as fast as I can till I get to the changing rooms.

I immediately see the door is ajar, but I decide the coach must have forgotten to lock it and I get in.

Then I realize I've made a mistake, but it's too late.

The two nerds are there. They're turning their backs on me and for a moment I hope I can steal away before they see me. But the blond bloke swivels round and catches me just as I'm creeping away.

"Oh, see who's there!" he sneers.

I freeze on the spot. My heart hammers and my throat tightens. The bloke starts moving forward and I struggle to regain control edging backward and trying to get to the door, but the red crested nerd slips behind me and bangs the door shut. I sprint to one side but the fair-haired bloke is over me now and pins me to the wall, his arms stretched out on both sides of my face. I curl up and the jerk starts howling with laughter. He assails me with the blast of his putrid breath.

"Where's the dough?" he hisses, putting his mouth against my ear.

I try to say something but I can't. My mind has gone blank.

"Lost his tongue?" the other nerd breaks in. "Do you think he needs our special treatment?"

I recover my voice at once. "Please," I plead in a hoarse whisper, knees shaking. "Please... I haven't got the money today. Couldn't find any. Next time, I promise."

The nerd's eyes widen. "Next time you said? And what about last week? You gave us nothing last week! We didn't even see you! Why didn't we see you?"

The nerd's voice is getting louder and louder and I feel like I'm shrinking. "Next time I'll give you more." I promise, my eyes filling with tears.

"Oh... hear that!" The nerd's dilated eyes are so close to mine now that I can spot the reddish threads of his veins swimming in a yellowish sea. "Of course you're giving us more... Next time make it fifty Euros, you little idiot! And stick this well in your head!" The nerd thrusts his forefinger into my chest and I curl up again. I feel warm dampness spreading down my legs. Suddenly there's a noise outside.

"Let's beat it!" The red crested jerk splutters.

The fair-haired nerd grabs my ear and twists it. Tears of pain come to my eyes. "We've got to go now," he hisses "but you keep your mouth shut and don't forget the dough. "

"I... I won't." I stammer, tears all over my face.

"And this is top secret, or..." he mimics throat slashing and I am openly sobbing now. "I... I won't... tell anyone." I stammer

"Come on!!! We've got to go!" the red-crested nerd urges.

The fair-haired bloke releases his hold on me and they both rush to the back door.

I slump to the floor.

A peal of laughter drips in through the window. The coach says something and there's some more laughter. I look at my tracksuit bottoms. There's a big wet spot on the front. Bullshit! I did it in my pants!

I pull myself up as fast as I can. I grab my bag and rush to the showers stripping off and flinging my clothes into it as I go. Half a second later I'm under a shower of icy water.

Keeping Watch

I'm

still here by the fence.

My eyes are closed, so it looks as if I'm sleeping. As a matter of fact, I'm keeping watch.

Haven't I heard the noise of a car coming right now?

I squint up into the sunlight.

Right! I can see that a car has just pulled up in front of the gate.

Luckily, it isn't our gate. It's our neighbour's. No obligation for me to bark.

Birillo should do it! But there's no trace of him. I bet he's fast asleep inside.

On second thoughts... I'd better go and have a look. Even though it's our neighbour's house, it's best to find out what's going on.

It's a waste of energy, I know, and I wouldn't be obliged to do it. But better safe than sorry, I think.

I get up with a yawn. Then I stretch a bit, scratch my neck, lick my tummy and after that I take a few steps forward.

There's a long, shining car in front of our neighbour's gate.

The car door opens and a man wearing a cap gets out. Then an elderly lady with a hat on her head gets out, too. There's a BIRD on the lady's hat!

The elderly lady with the bird on her hat rings the bell.

Before anyone from the house turns up, a girl with

a long ponytail jumps out of the car.

The girl, the man and the elderly lady stand still, waiting.

I stand still, too, wondering. The problem is I can't smell those people very well from here... I'd better move on a bit...

I start moving towards the gate but a piercing scream freezes me midway. It's our neighbour. She's opened the door and she's screaming like mad as she runs to the gate.

Then she stops in front of the girl and hugs her tightly. She starts sobbing.

The girl stands still looking embarrassed.

In the end, our neighbour dries her tears on her sleeve, shakes hands with the old lady and greets the man.

The man touches his cap and bows. Then he opens the car door for the elderly lady with the bird on her hat to get in.

The elderly lady gets in, the man shuts the door, touches his cap again, gets into the car and starts the engine.

The car pulls away and in a matter of seconds it disappears from sight.

Only the young girl has been left on the ground.

Plus two big suitcases.

Birillo appears at the door.

The girl runs to him.

Birillo starts trembling like a leaf in the wind, wildly shaking the stupid red ribbon on his head.

The girl gets down on her knees and starts patting him on the head.

I'm green with envy.

Barefoot On The Grass

I'm still here by the fence. I'm staring at a couple of bees swimming in front of my eyes. They circle around my head and now and then one or the other comes closer and sits on my nose making it twitch. With a good snap I might make a mouthful of them, but I don't really care for bee food.

I wonder what I'm waiting for. I seem to have forgotten right now, but I'm sure it'll come to mind sooner or later.

All of a sudden I hear a shuffling sound and I can smell mint and wild flowers. I open my eyes and I see the girl. She's standing barefoot on the grass on the other side of the fence and she's staring at me. I stare at her, too, and we go on staring at each other for a while.

In the end the girl says: "What a beautiful dog you are!"

I jump up and go to the fence, my tail wagging wildly. I adore compliments.

I push my nose into the wire net and the girl strokes it gently with her fingers. I'm very partial to people who stroke my nose.

"What's your name?" the girl asks.

I wag my tail and bark softly.

"My name is Giselle." she says.

I keep wagging my tail and barking softly. Out of the corner of my eye I see the gate open and the car pull into the driveway. It stops in front of the garage. Tommy gets out and starts walking towards me.

I remember now! It was Tommy I was waiting for!

I leave the girl and run to him. I jump up and place my legs on his shoulders. Then I rush back to the fence where the girl is waiting. I want Tommy to see her at once!

But Tommy isn't coming. He's stopped midway and he's just staring at us. How's that?

I stick out my tongue and wag my tail, but Tommy is stuck to the ground. Why isn't he coming? Hasn't he seen the girl?

I run to him again, then back to the girl.

Then back to him, then back to the girl again.

Tommy stands still. He looks as stiff as a broomstick.

Luckily, it's Giselle who starts the conversation. "Hallo! Is this your dog?" she asks. "He's such a beautiful big dog! And very friendly, isn't he? What's his name? My name is Giselle, by the way. What's your name?"

Tommy is dumbfounded. Then, at last, he stutters: "Teodorico... Teo... Tommy... Tommaso. " He stops and gulps. Then he says: "Tommy is my name and Teo is the dog's name... "

"They're both nice names!" Giselle says with a grin. "I had a cat called Madame Mirabò in Paris, but I never had a dog, even though I so much wanted one..."

"Paris?" asks Tommy.

"Yes, I've just come over from Paris. I'm staying with my aunt... and you live here, don't you?"

"Ha, ha. Are you staying for the summer?"

"Well, actually, it could be more than just the summer."

"Really?"

The girl nods. Then, for some reason, she suddenly looks gloomy. "I might stay longer than just the summer." she repeats, pulling a face. Then she brightens up again and asks: "And what about you? Aren't you going away on holiday?"

"I don't think so."

"Really? That's fantastic!" the girl shouts.

Tommy blushes and I start barking. They both jump in surprise and stare at me. Then they burst into laughter.

"That's a good boy." Tommy says, patting my head.

"I bet he wants to join the conversation." Giselle says.

"Tommaso!!! Where are you now?"

That was Marianna's voice coming from the kitchen. What a nag! Tommy rolls his eyes and does not answer.

"Tommaso!"

Tommy takes a big sigh and then he cries: "Yes, mum!?"

"What are you doing there? Come inside and get changed if you want to stay in the garden!"

Tommy frowns. "Got to go." he says "But I'll be back at once. "

"I'll wait."

"I won't be long."

"OK"

Tommy runs away and I stay with the girl. She sits down on the grass on the other side of the fence, her legs crossed. I sit down on the grass, too. The girl starts chatting and I prick up my ears.

She says that having a dog like me has been the dream of her life... that Birillo refused to come out of the house and went to sleep on her aunt's bed... that our garden is so charming, much more charming than her garden in Paris... that she likes our garden because it looks so wild, so natural, so mysterious...

For a second she stops talking and squints her eyes as if she were trying to better understand her idea of a mystery garden. Then she starts talking again and she goes on and on until her words mix with the humming of bees, the buzzing of bottlenecks, the twitter of birds, the croaking of frogs, the chirping of crickets...

I can't help getting distracted a bit but then, all of a

sudden, something she says makes me prick up my ears. Did she really say she wants to make a hole in the fence?

Right at that moment Tommy turns up and asks the question for me. "Did I hear you say you want to make a hole in the net?"

Giselle startles. "You gave me such a fright!" she says. Then she shrugs. "Well, I was talking to Teodorico, and that was just an idea I had."

Tommy frowns. "The idea of making a hole in the fence?"

"Yes."

"Why?"

"Well, if there was a hole, I'd be able to get through."

Tommy frowns again. "Can't you come in through the gate?"

"Of course I can! But that wouldn't be real fun, would it? I mean... imagine my having to ask permission every time I want to come! I know what aunt Camilla would say: now you can't because you have to do this... now you can't because I want you to do that..."

Giselle stops talking to get her breath back and then she starts again: "You know, it took me ages to convince aunt Camilla to let me come out by myself. She's a real nitpicker about what I can do and how I must do it."

"I see." Tommy closes his mouth after keeping it open during the whole speech.

"If we make a hole where the fence is hidden inside the hedge, no one will ever find out." the girl says.

Tommy keeps silent.

"There's quite a large area covered with bushes over there! That might be the right place, don't you think so?"

Tommy doesn't answer. I can see he's intently looking at Giselle's bare feet now.

"Can you see what I mean? Over there! Look! There

are thick bushes on both sides of the fence. Wouldn't that be the perfect place?"

Finally Tommy finds his tongue. "Perfect for what?"

"For making a secret hole in the fence!"

Tommy rolls his eyes. "But the vegetation is so thick over there! It was meant to be just a hedge but Dad never found the time to trim it so it's full of brambles now. How do you think we can get through?"

"We can cut the vegetation at ground level so as to make a sort of tunnel. See what I mean?"

Tommy shakes his head but Giselle doesn't seem to mind. "Let's go and have a look, shall we?" she says. After that she runs to the end of the garden. We go there too. We can no longer see her now, as she's disappeared behind the bushes on the other side of the fence, but we can hear her. "I think this is the right place. We can make a tunnel on both sides." she says.

Tommy shrugs and gives in. "OK. I'll get the

shears."

"Shears?"

"Yes, to cut the vegetation with."

"Good idea! I'll be waiting."

Tommy goes and nothing else happens for a while. I sit down again and I close my eyes.

Then, all of a sudden I hear the snap of twigs being broken. I jump up and see the upper part of the bushes on the other side of the fence waving as if they were shaken by some sort of strong wind.

Tommy is back now. "Are you still there?" he shouts.

"Shush! Don't shout please or they'll hear us!" Giselle's voice now comes from under the bushes. "I've gone inside for an inspection. "

"Aren't we going to make the tunnel?" Tommy asks.

"Of course we are!" Giselle says.

There's some more waving of branches and some more snaps of broken twigs, then we finally see Giselle again. Her hair is a mess and there are smears of dirt on her hands and knees.

"I hope there aren't any snakes under those bushes." Tommy says.

"I didn't see any. I only saw a few spiders." Giselle says brushing a lock of hair off her forehead. Now there's a smear of dirt on her face as well.

"Let me give you the shears then. Look out! I'm going to throw them to you." Tommy says.

Giselle moves backwards and the shears fly above the fence. She picks them up. "Let's start at once, shall we?"

I can see that making a tunnel is not an easy job at all! Tommy is on his fours now. He's working hard cutting twigs, moaning and sucking his fingers every time he gets pricked by the thorns. I sit at the back and move forward behind him. At last we can see Giselle and in a matter of seconds only the wire net divides us. Tommy and Giselle look at each other. Then they start laughing. "We've made it!" Tommy says.

"Tommy! Where are you?"

Oh, no! That was Marianna again! And her voice was SO NEAR! We hold our breath and keep still. A few seconds later we start breathing again because the voice has moved away. "Tooommy! Where are you? Lunch is ready!"

"Phew! I thought she was going to catch us out." Tommy says. "I've got to go now."

"I'd better go, too. Aunt Camilla should be coming back from the supermarket any moment. She'll throw a fit if she doesn't find me at home."

"Let's come back here after lunch, shall we?"

"OK."

"I'm going then."

"So am I."

Neither of them moves.

"Woof!" I say, just to say something.

"Shut up!" Giselle and Tommy say at one voice. Then they start laughing. I don't know why.

The Den

Actually,

lunch was not really ready yet and I had to wait quite a bit. Then Mum said she didn't feel like eating and she left me alone in front of my spaghetti.

Now I'm gulping the food as usual. I've become a fast eater because I can play video-games from after lunch until three o'clock and from after dinner until half past nine. So, the quicker I eat, the longer I can play. Today I have a different reason for eating fast.

As soon as I've finished I try to slip away but Mum sees me. She's on the phone and she puts a hand on the microphone. "Where are you going?" she asks. She has a strange voice. I peer at her and I think she looks tense.

"I'm... I'm just going out... into the... the garden, I mean." I stutter. I have a tendency to stutter when I don't feel at ease.

Mum frowns. "Won't it be too hot?"

"I don't think so."

"No video-games today?"

"Well, I'd rather get some fresh air."

"Fresh air?" Mum stares at me, but then she gets distracted by what the other person is saying on the phone and I rush out.

As soon as I get out of the door I'm struck by a tremendous wave of heat. I look around. There's no trace of Teo. How funny! He always sleeps by the door when I'm inside. Where has he gone now? Well, I bet I know where he is... he must be with Giselle, of course.

I head for the hedge and as soon as I get to the bushes, Teo comes out of the tunnel wagging his tail. I yell at him: "Here you are, then! I've been looking for you!"

Teo grins and pants, his tail wagging faster than usual. Then he swivels round and goes back into the hole. I get down on my fours and start crawling behind him.

When I get to the fence I see Giselle is already there. She's all flushed. "Here you are at last!" she cries. "Teo and I have been waiting for ages!"

"Well... I had to have lunch! Didn't you have any lunch?

"Of course, I did."

"You were very quick then."

"I never eat much."

"Don't you? And what did your aunt say? I mean, didn't you say she doesn't want you to stay out on your own?"

Giselle shrugs. "Actually, I had no problems at all! Aunt Camilla switched on the TV and started watching a soap opera with Birillo. Two minutes later they were both fast asleep. So I didn't even have to ask. I hope she's not going to wake up soon."

"Doesn't your aunt have to go to work?"

Giselle takes a deep sigh, then she says: "Of course she does, but she's on holiday for the whole month, unfortunately, and..."

"And?"

Giselle pulls a face. "She said she'll be looking for a babysitter."

"A babysitter? What for?"

Giselle frowns. "To look after me when she goes back to work next month! Can you imagine that?"

"I'm sure she'll change her mind once she's got to know you better."

"Hmm... I don't know..."

I keep silent. Then Giselle says: "Let's go on with our job now that you're here."

"Right! What we have to do now is just cut the wire..." I say.

I find the shears I left on the ground and I try them out on the wire. Oh, bother! It's tough! I clasp the handles with both hands and press them as tightly as I can. I tighten my lips and clench my teeth in the effort. At last the wire breaks with a click. Phew!

"Tough work!" Giselle says.

Awful, actually!

"I can manage." I say.

Click after click, I make the hole bigger and bigger even though my hands hurt, my fingers hurt and even my teeth hurt out of clenching them tightly.

While I'm working, Giselle keeps chatting. She says her ears got blocked at take off... *I've never been on a plane myself...* that the hut she built with Hervé in the garden had two rooms... *I wonder who Hervé is...* that Madame Mirabò tried to scratch her every time she wanted to cuddle her but she's missing her all the same... that she's worried because she doesn't even know who she ended up with and if she's happy with her new family... *I wouldn't bother so much for a scratching cat if I were her...* that Birillo sleeps all the time... *I know of another dog who could beat a record at sleeping...* that her new room is so sad and empty! Just a bed, a wardrobe and the desk... that she'd hoped to find all her books in it but they haven't arrived yet, even though she sent them two days before she left Paris... *how can anyone feel nostalgic about books?* That aunt Camilla cries secretly... that she's sure she does, because she sometimes has red rimmed eyes and she often clutches a hanky... *This is funny! I had always thought of Ms Doroni as such a cheerful lady...*

Giselle goes on talking and talking. I'm in a sweat and I can't feel my hands any more, but finally the hole is big enough for us to get through.

"Now I can come through." Giselle says.

"Right!" I say.

I start moving backwards on my fours and Giselle

starts crawling after me. When we get out of the tunnel at last and we stand up, I realize Giselle is a bit taller than me. Two or three centimetres at least. And she's barefoot besides!

"How old are you?" I ask.

"I'm eleven and three months old. And you?"

"Eleven, two months and a half."

I wonder if I'll be able to grow up to her height in half a month. "What are we going to do now?" I ask.

Giselle lowers her eyes and stares at her feet. Then she starts twisting a lock of hair around her finger. As she's not looking at me now, I can take a closer look at her. Her thin hair is so pale that it looks almost white under the sun. Also her lowered eyelashes are thin and whitish against the net of freckles on her cheeks and nose. All of a sudden she looks up and I startle, lowering my eyes.

"We ought to go on with the job now."

Go on with the job? What job? I wipe my brow with

the back of my hand. I'm soaking wet with sweat.

I'm not going to do any other job! Not on your life!

"What kind of job?" I ask.

"I was looking at the thicket of brambles over there... It looks like a small wood, doesn't it?"

I turn to look at the spot she's pointing to. There's another thick mess of tall brambles at the end of the garden. Dad keeps saying he'll clear everything up one of these days, but he never does.

"That thicket would be perfect." Giselle says.

What's she talking about?

"Perfect for what?"

"As a hiding place."

Is she nuts or what?

"Are you saying you want to hide in my garden?"

"Yes, I'd like to."

"What for?"

"Well... I don't know... We might need to hide somewhere sooner or later and that little wood would be a perfect hiding place, wouldn't it?"

She's definitely nuts!

"That's not a bad idea." I say.

"I know what we can do." Giselle declares. "We can cut another tunnel along the fence so as to be able to get into the thicket without having to get out of the bushes! In this way we would be under cover all the time!"

Under cover? Cutting one more tunnel? Thorns and heat and I don't know what else! Ants and even snakes, perhaps. I'm sick and tired of this stupid game!

"OK. Let's make another tunnel." I say.

Giselle jumps for joy and in no time we're back near the hole in the fence. I get the shears and set down to work.

There's a suffocating heat under the bushes. I'm all in a sweat, smeared with dirt and awfully itching all over.

Each twig I cut is full of stinging thorns. Then come the ants, as I had foreseen. Luckily, not those small ants with a red head that go to the jam. These are big black ants and they do not seem to sting.... but I'd rather they didn't crawl all over my arms, neck and legs! Anyway, I keep to my job stoically, while Giselle continues her chattering. Now she's telling me about her school in Paris which lasted all day... a*ll day? Poor her! I 'd die if I had to stay at school all day!*... of the ghost stories her granny used to tell her at night until she fell asleep... *ghost stories? Wow!*... of her large house in Paris and of her bedroom filled with books... *books again!*

I suddenly stop cutting because I've realized there aren't any twigs close to my face now. I look up and see that we've got to a sort of small clearing. We both stand up. The vegetation brushes our heads and we have to duck a little, but Giselle is thrilled. "How nice! This is just like a natural hut!" she cries. Then she kneels down and shouts: "Look here! Now I know why there's a clearing!

There must have been some big trees standing close to one another, which were then cut at the base. The stumps have prevented the bushes from growing. Can you see?"

I bend down to have a proper look and we both start removing the carpet of dead leaves with our hands. Below the leaves we can spot round wooden surfaces, the clear remains of cut tree trunks. They're not at exactly the same height, so the ground is rather uneven and between the stumps there are some rocks and an outgrowth of dwarf bushes. Anyway, on the whole this looks like a sort of rough wooden floor.

"This is wonderful!" Giselle says in a dreamy voice. She is now lying on her back, her arms open. "It's not that comfortable." she admits after a moment, shuffling around a bit.

I lie down near her and something spiky pricks my back. I shuffle around and the spike disappears, but now my head sinks. I look upwards and my eyes meet the roof of leaves quivering over our heads. Above the leaves the tiny spots of blue sky look so very far away... the still air seems to absorb every noise. I feel as if I have suddenly plunged into a different world.

"You know... we might come here every day." Giselle says quietly.

I close my eyes and decide to keep silent.

"This might become our secret hut. I wonder what it would be like to come here at night."

Coming here at night? What a silly thing to say!

"Why at night?" I ask, turning my head to look at her profile. She has a small upturned nose sprinkled with freckles and she looks so very sad now. Why does she suddenly look so sad, I wonder?

"Would you be scared?" she asks without looking at me.

I'm taken aback. "Of course, not!" I blatantly lie.

"We might bring a blanket, biscuits, fruit, our

favourite books..."

I roll my eyes. "And the fridge, the TV, the computer, the stereo..."

Giselle turns to look at me. She has big, deep eyes in a very unusual shade of blue, almost violet. I look away and try to think of something else to say, but my mind seems to have gone blank. After a while I come out with: "You said you come from Paris?"

"I did."

"So, if you are French, how is it that you don't speak French?"

"But I do speak French!"

"But you also speak Italian!"

"That's because I'm half Italian. Only my father was French. Both my mother and my Granny were Italian and I went to an Italian school."

"An Italian school in Paris?

"Yes."

I keep silent for a while, thinking about all the past tenses she's used to talk about her family. A cold shiver runs down my spine. "So you can speak both French and Italian."

"Huh, huh."

"Say something in French, then."

"What do you want me to say?"

"Anything you want."

Giselle sighs and then she says: "jesiuìtanuvellamì"

It sounds funny and it makes me chuckle. Then I ask: "What does that mean?"

"It means: I am your new friend."

I catch my breath and blush scarlet. It takes me a few moments but I finally pluck up my courage and I quickly say: "And I'm your new friend."

"Thank you." Giselle says quietly. Then she takes a big sigh. "I need to go back home now before aunt Camilla wakes up. You won't tell anyone about this place, will you?"

"Of course not! Why should I?"

 "What about saying this is our Den?"

"Fine."

I'm still shocked at the idea of coming here at night so I don't any longer feel like talking much. Giselle keeps silent, too. She seems to be deep in thought now. I wonder what she's thinking about. At last she asks: "Where's Teo?"

I pull myself up and look around. Teo is not in sight. This is not like him as he sticks to me all the time. I whistle for him, but nothing happens. I whistle again. This time we can hear shuffling and rustling then Teo shows up, his muzzle all smeared with dirt and something whitish in his mouth.

"Where have you been? What's that?" I ask, moving forward.

Teo backs up whipping his head around and curling his lip.

Giselle goes to him, too. This time Teo does not stir.

"It's a bone." Giselle says. "It's an old bone all covered with earth."

"Yuck! I wonder where he found it!"

Madame Mirabò

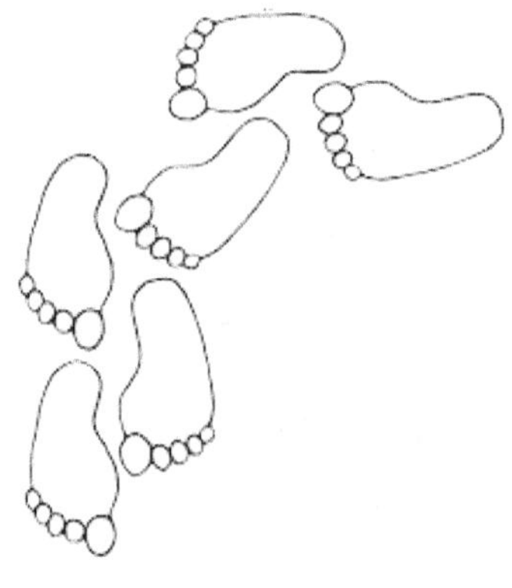

I'm

walking along a corridor
with many doors on both
sides, all of them shut.
The walls are decorated
with large mirrors
where I can see
numberless reflections of myself.
I must have been walking a long time

as I feel awfully tired.
I'd so much like to lie down and sleep
but there's no place where I can stop,
so I keep going.
I hope I'll sooner or later
end up somewhere.
I suddenly realize that huge pictures
have taken the place of the mirrors now.
I stop in front of the portrait
of a lady in a white wig,
a beauty spot on her cheek
and a fan in her hand.
As I look at the picture
the lady suddenly starts fanning her face.
I can't believe my eyes
and I keep watching
to make sure I'm not dreaming.
Then the lady suddenly smiles at me.
"What can I do to help you?"

she asks in a soft voice.
This scares me out of my wits
and I dart forward
but, before I can take flight,
the lady jumps out of her portrait
and stands in front of me
barring my way.
"I do not think it is very polite
to run away
without asking permission
or even saying goodbye,
young man."
the lady says,
shaking her finger at me.
Even though I'm shivering all over
I manage to find my voice
and I stammer:
"I'm very sorry, Mrs... Miss..."

"You may call me
Madame Mirabò"
the lady says.
"Excuse me, Madame Mirabò,
I was wondering
if you could tell me
how to get out of this place."
I say in one breath.
"It all depends
where you would like to go, young man."
a voice says.
I swivel round and I see
that a gentleman in a wig
is peering at me
through his monocle
from a big portrait on my left.
"If you would like to go left,
for example, you should turn left."
the gentleman explains in a grave voice.

84

"And if you would like to go right,
you should turn right..."
declares a fat woman
in a pink dress and white lace
from a portrait on my right.
"If you would like to go downstairs
you should go down the stairs..."
adds Madame Mirabò.
"And if you would like to go upstairs
you should..."
"Go up the stairs, I bet!"
I snap, turning to look
at a stern man with a long beard
who is scowling at me
from another big picture.
"Don't be so rude, young man!"
says Madame Mirabò
shaking her finger again.

"Sorry, I didn't mean to be rude at all!
The fact is I really need
to get out of this place!
I'm sick and tired of being stuck here
but I can't see a way out!"
"That is probably because
you are not doing the right thing,
young man!" Madame Mirabò says.
"And what's the right thing to do?"
"This is quite hard to say,
but I suggest that you should get going!
Staying here will not help you."
says the man with the monocle.
"The sooner you get going the better!"
says Madame Mirabò.
"Is that all?" I ask.
"I'm very disappointed, I must say!
As old and wise as you are,
I did hope you would be able

"Let me give you some good advice before it's too late! If you don't get out of my way I'll give you a taste of this rake!"

I open my eyes. That was Dad's voice mixing up with my dream. He's yelling at Teo for a change.

What time is it? Eight o'clock, already? I thought it was earlier. There's such a gloomy light in the room!

I get out of bed. I go to the window to look at the sky. It's all covered, but it doesn't look like rain. Not near at hand, at least. And even if it rained, there wouldn't be any hope for the match to be put off. Not even a thunderstorm would be a good enough reason.

I look at Dad who is mowing the lawn. Teo is furiously barking at the lawn-mower, backing up when the mower moves forward and darting forward when it moves back. Dad keeps yelling at him.

I suddenly remember that the match is at our football ground today and my heart sinks because this means I'll have to face The Two.

I need to think of something I might say to convince Mum and Dad to let me stay at home. My head starts buzzing with ideas but none of them looks really convincing.

What time is it again? Three minutes past eight. I'll have to be ready in less than half an hour.

I decide to go downstairs before getting dressed. What if I made one more try with Mum? I might tell her I feel awfully sick, that my throat's on fire, that my head's splitting... anything will be better than nothing, I decide.

But when I get to the kitchen, Mum is not in sight. What I immediately set my eyes on, instead, is Dad's wallet, in full view on the table.

I open it. There are several banknotes inside. Twenty and fifty Euro notes. I'd never seen so many!

Without giving myself the time to think, I slip a fifty Euro note out of the wallet, I put the wallet back on the table, then I pick it up again and take out a second note. I thrust the two banknotes into my pyjama pocket and I rush upstairs. I slip into bed and try to calm down my thumping heart.

Not a minute has passed when Mum calls me. "Tommy, are you still sleeping?

I keep silent. If I pretend to be sleeping I'll have a perfect alibi.

I hear the noise of mum's steps on the stairs.

"Tommy!"

When Mum gets into my room I don't stir and when she calls me again I slowly sit up blinking sleepily. Then I repeatedly rub my eyes and yawn.

"What a sleepyhead you are!" Mum says, sitting on the bed near me. "If you don't come down for breakfast at once you'll be late for the match."

"OK." I mutter, yawning again.

From the garden I can still hear the buzzing noise of the lawn-mower, the furious barking of Teo and Dad's yells.

CHAPTER THREE

(Saturday, 16th July)

Daydreaming

Teo and I have been waiting for Giselle in the Den for over an hour, but she hasn't turned up yet. After the morning's rain, the sky is clear again. The sun filters through the wet leaves, making the tiny raindrops glimmer and sending patterns of flickering shadows all around. I'm lying on the ground and Teo is sleeping, for a change. He must be having a nightmare as he's panting and whining and shaking. I pat him on the head and he calms down.

I close my eyes and I see myself in the soccer field...

I'm one of the regular players today.

I've come off the bench at last

and this is because...

Let's say it's because...

the other two reserves were absent?

So the coach didn't have

any other choice but let me play.

No, better say that the coach

picked me because he thinks

I can do really well.

So I am in the field, playing defence,

I mean, playing attack.

We're losing one-nil

and there's not much time left.

"I know you can make it."

said the coach

before sending me in,

a hand on my shoulder.

Baldini is now dribbling

near the penalty area.

He sees me and passes the ball.

I get it and dribble past two... three...

four defenders,

heading for the net,

then I chip the ball

making it fly to the left

of the goalie's head.

The goalie jumps up a second too late

and the ball drops down

behind his back.

It's a goal!!!

A GOOOAAALLL!!!

Now it's a draw one-one

and I've scored MY FIRST GOAL!!!

The first goal IN MY LIFE!

I CAN'T BELIEVE IT!

All our supporters are standing up now,

whooping and hollering.

With the corner of my eye

I see Mum and Dad

clapping their hands,

happy smiles on their faces.

I know they're so proud of me!

They wave at me

then they smile at each other

and kiss on the mouth.

Yuck!

"Hallo!"

I jump up, bang my head against a low branch and sit down again. Teo wakes up and starts bouncing.

"I didn't hear you come." I say, rubbing my head.

"Were you sleeping?"

"Not really! I was thinking."

"Have you been waiting long?"

"No... yes, I did."

"I wanted to come earlier, but I couldn't."

"It doesn't matter, really! I was just having a rest."

"Why? Are you tired? What have you been doing?"

"A match."

"What kind of match?"

"Soccer."

"Oh, that's fantastic! I didn't know you played soccer. Did you win?"

"Well, it was pouring this morning and, actually, no, we didn't win. We lost two-nil."

"What a shame!"

I shrug. "Oh, well, I don't mind, really... I didn't even play, anyway."

"Why?"

"I wasn't well."

"I see..."

Giselle is now staring at me so sternly that I find it impossible to look away. I suddenly feel the need to tell the truth. "Actually, I didn't play because I'm... well... I'm a real bungler, you know... I'm a reserve."

"A reserve?"

"Yes, I sit on the bench looking at the others play."

"Oh, but that must be pretty boring! So you sat on the bench under the rain during the whole match?"

"I did." I know I look utterly dejected and I really am. It's the first time I've ever spoken about this and it hurts more than just thinking about it. I'm feeling miserable.

Giselle frowns and then she shakes her head. "I wouldn't like that at all!" she declares. Then she asks: "Is it that difficult to play well?"

I shrug. "Probably not. But I seem to be totally hopeless."

"Isn't there someone who can teach you?"

"Of course! The coach is trying to teach me, but I'll

never learn."

"But you'd like to learn, wouldn't you?"

"Of course I would!"

Giselle drops flat on her back. I steal a glance at her because she's stopped talking. She's staring at the canopy of leaves over our heads and she appears to be deep in thought now. Then she suddenly comes back to earth.

"You know what?" she says sitting up and glaring at me with her violet-blue eyes. "I think I've something that might help you!"

"Help me do what?"

"Learn how to play soccer."

"What is it?"

"A book."

"A book on how to play soccer?"

"Not exactly ..."

"So?"

"It's a book on magic." she says.

"A book on magic? You're kidding, aren't you?"

"I'm not."

"So YOU believe in MAGIC?"

"Well, I don't, actually, but... well, yes, in a way I do." Giselle mutters.

"Do you or don't you?"

Giselle shakes her head. "I know magic works."

"Come on! You're not being serious!"

I know for sure a book is of no use for teaching someone how to play soccer... and a book on magic besides!   Is she nuts or what?

"Magic can work sometimes. It happened to me, you know. "

"What?"

"This book I was telling you about... Granny had given it to me. She'd told me magic was just for fun but, you know, I once tried it and it worked."

I gawk at her. "Really?"

Giselle nods. "I lost my locket, once. This one, you see?" she reaches for a thin golden chain she's wearing around her neck.

I look at the chain closely and I see there's a small locket hanging from it.

"I was out of my mind. The locket was on the chain and the next minute it had vanished into thin air. I had no idea where to look and I was desperate for days... Then, one day, I came across this book I was telling you about and I got so involved I couldn't stop reading. In the end I cast the spell and two minutes later I found it."

"What did you find?"

"Why, the locket!"

"Did you find the locket after casting the spell?"

"Yes!"

"And where did you find it?"

"It had slipped between the sofa and the wall. Now I

know it must have happened while I was playing with Madame Mirabò, but..."

I shake my head. "I don't see any magic in this."

"But I do! I might have lost the locket forever if I hadn't thought of looking in the right place!"

I fall silent.

"You don't believe me, do you? You don't even want to try!" she says. There's an accusatory note in her voice and she looks so terribly serious now. I suddenly wonder why this locket is so important to her. I don't dare ask, though.

"Well, actually, I was just thinking I might." I hear myself say.

I'm so surprised at what I've said that I can't help flushing deeply. Luckily, Giselle doesn't seem to notice as she's lying on her back again, looking up at the roof of leaves.

"Good." she says after a while. "You know what the problem is, though? We don't have enough time during the day."

"Huh?"

"Aunt Camilla keeps watch on me all the time, you know. If she can't see me for more than two minutes she starts yelling."

"So, how can you stay here now?"

"That's because she's gone to church, to her charity she said, with a bunch of second-hand clothes. She said she'll be back for dinner."

"Clothes?"

"Yes, she's involved in this charity thing. She collects used clothes, she washes and repairs them, then she takes them to the second-hand shop at the parish and the money she makes from the sales goes to charity."

"That's very good of her! So we can wait for another chance like this."

"Hmm... I'm not so sure... it might take long before she stays out the whole afternoon again. You know what?

I think we should do it tonight. The sooner the better, don't you think so?"

TONIGHT?

"I can bring a blanket, a torch and something to eat. And you should bring a piece of paper and a pen. You'll have to take notes."

"Take notes?"

"Yes. You'll need to take notes if you want to remember how to make the spell. It's not so easy, you know."

"Couldn't I just borrow your book?"

"No."

"I wouldn't spoil it or lose it or anything!"

"I know, but I simply can't give the book away. Not even for a few hours. Besides you'd need my help all the same. It's an old book, you see... it's written in a strange language."

"Is it in French?"

"No, it's in Italian, but all the same..."

I keep silent. I'll never get out of bed at night, that I know for sure.

"OK. Let's do it." I hear myself say.

"Really?"

"Yes, but not tonight!"

"Well, it doesn't have to be tonight. Aunt Camilla takes a sleeping pill every night, so it could be any night."

I shiver.

"Are you scared?"

I startle. "I'm not scared but... well, the fact is I don't believe in magic, that's all!"

Phew! I've spoken my mind at last. I look at Giselle from the corner of my eye just to see her reaction, but she's still staring at the leaves.

"I've got to go now. See you." I sit up, get on all fours and start crawling through the tunnel without looking back. I know I'm running away and I'm sure Giselle is thinking I'm being rude.

"If you change your mind put a note by the hole in the net." Giselle shouts at my back.

I pretend not to hear her and keep crawling.

Then I realize that Teo is not following me. I turn and see he still sitting next to Giselle and he's staring at me, his ears cocked and his head tilted. I bet he's wondering why I'm running away.

"Come on, Teo. Come with me." I say.

But Teo doesn't stir.

THE TRAITOR!

CHAPTER FOUR

(Sunday, 17th July)

Bread and Salami

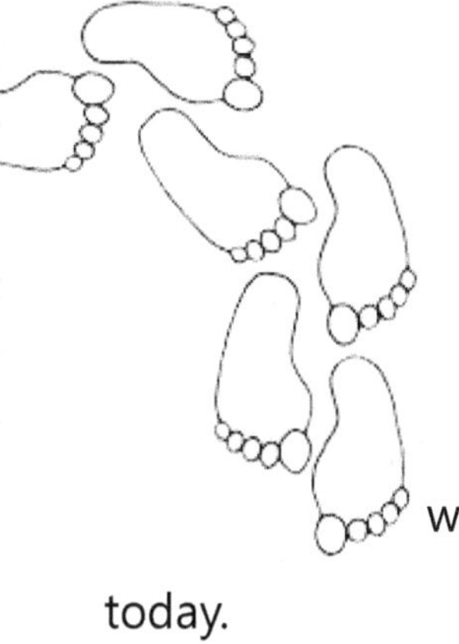

Such an awful day, today! I'm exhausted.

Last night I couldn't believe my ears when Dad said we'd be going on a hike today.

They woke me up so early I couldn't keep my eyes open, so when Mum said I was to put on my corduroy long shorts because they were right for the mountain, I didn't have the strength to protest and now I'm itching all over.

And if I think how long I had to climb! Over an hour, before we got to the top. There were moments when I thought I'd lie down and die.

The only good thing now is that Dad and Mum have finally stopped arguing, or discussing, as they put it.

It's funny how their rows always start at weekends. But that's probably because they have more time, being busy as they are during the week.

It's

been such a FANTASTIC DAY today! I would never have guessed it would be so nice, seeing how it started.

This morning, Corrado was already bustling about when the sun hadn't risen yet, a storm on his face.

Marianna kept going back and forth like a bear with a soar head, while Tommy was standing near the car. He looked fast asleep to me.

When I moved closer for a better look, Corrado barked at me furiously: "Go away, you silly dog!"

I walked away but Tommy suddenly came out of hibernation and shouted: "Come back here, Teo!"

I hesitantly started walking back, but Marianna stopped me immediately. "The dog is not coming!" she declared.

I started walking away again, then Tommy shouted: "Why not?"

"Because he smells!"

"He doesn't! If Teo isn't coming I'm not coming either."

I kept turning my head from one to the other to see who was going to win the battle and after a little I sneezed. I always sneeze when I'm nervous.

"And he's got a cold, besides!" Marianna shouted.

"He hasn't!" Tommy shouted back.

"He'll be shedding fleas all over the car!"

"He won't!"

Between a hot and a cold blow it was Tommy who won at last. But, in the meantime, I had made up my mind not to go. A disturbing association of ideas between going by car and going to the vet had suddenly struck me. So I decided to sneak away before it was too late. Luckily, Tommy understood what I had in mind, clutched me by the collar and pulled me towards the car. Even though I immediately adopted the frozen dog tactic, he somehow managed to put me in the boot.

Luckily, as I said! Just think what I would have missed if I hadn't gone! That was clear to me as soon as I put my nose in and I found myself swimming in a sea of delicious salami smells! Like those luscious smells from the closet, but much closer at hand!

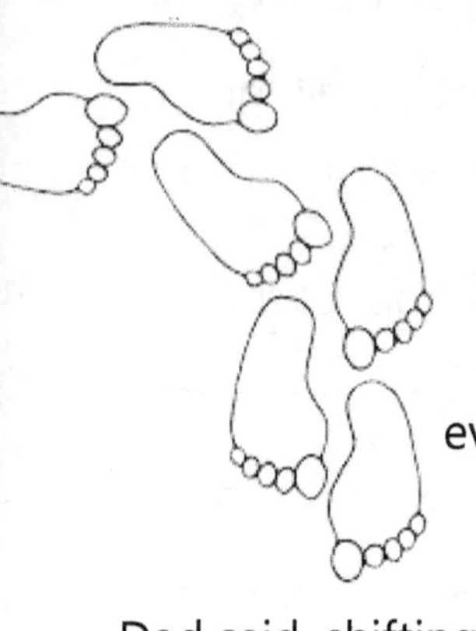

"**C**an't you see that the dog is slobbering everywhere?" Mum complained.

"He's smelling the salami sandwiches." Dad said, shifting the rucksack from the boot to the empty seat on my side.

Teo followed the smell until his head was level with mine. He licked my neck and I tried to make him move away, but he wouldn't. He remained stuck on his four legs, slobbering on my shoulder all the time, a happy smile on his face, as if he was having the greatest fun. He didn't move even when the turnings started making him swing to and fro.

I hated those awful turnings. They made me feel sick all the time. If you add this to the fact that Mum and Dad had already started their first deafening "discussion" and that Teo kept slobbering over my shoulder and every now and then licked my neck, it's surprising that I could go back to sleep again.

Then, when we got to the village at the foot of the mountain where we left the car, we had the hen problem. Who would have ever imagined? As I opened the boot Teo darted out like a shot and in no time he was bouncing and barking amid a cloud of flying feathers and in an awful squawking of hens in flight.

It was quite hard to calm him down. Dad had to pick up a twig and break it on his back! The twig was not very thick, luckily, and it was half rotten, so I don't think it can have hurt him too much... that's what I hope, at least.

Anyway, the hens were safe and sound, or almost so. Some of their feathers were left on the battlefield, actually, but all of them were still on their legs when we stole away before the hens' owners turned up, with Teo on the leash.

What

the heck! I had almost set my teeth on two or three of those big birds when I got that painful blow on the back, damn it!

Then there was the leash problem.

I hate leashes. I get hot under the collar when I'm on a leash. So I tried almost all the tactics I know: sudden stop, tugging and drawing, pulling back, running and then suddenly halting... but it took a heck of a time before Tommy decided to let me go.

"I have to unleash him," he finally said "he's going to tear off my arm!"

About time he did!

As soon as I realized I was free, I ran ahead at full speed

without bothering about the calls: "Come back here, silly dog!" "Wait for us, Teo!" "Come back at once, stupid beast!"

How could I possibly listen to them? I was lost in a rhapsody of incredible smells: small black droppings, mint pee, savoury grass, mice, lizards, slobbering snails, spiders, wasps, bluebottles, sparrows, blackbirds and frogs... what a delicious smell of fresh frogs! Not so good as the smell of dry frogs I can smell on the road in front of our gate, but very interesting all the same. I'd never smelled so many good smells in all my life!

At last we came to an endless sloping lawn of thick grass. I slumped down flat and scratched my back.

Then I rolled down the slope and when I got to the bottom I gave myself to a thorough hunt of butterflies and wasps...

Then Tommy called: "Come back here, Teo! Come here, I said! We're eating!"

EATING? Eating did not sound familiar, as a word, in

the middle of the day! Anyway, it appeared promising, so I

ran back to the top and found them all sitting on the

grass, munching bread and salami. I must have looked

desperately hungry because they GAVE ME A SALAMI

SANDWICH! Incredible, isn't it? It was delicious!

*O*n

the way back I had to do a pooh

and I stopped near a bush. Mum and

Dad kept walking. They hadn't noticed I wasn't there,

busy as they were shouting at each other. Teo was not in

sight.

Then, right in the middle of my business, he suddenly

appeared and sat next to me, waiting.

When I was done, I started running so as to catch up with Mum and Dad but soon Teo grabbed me by the back of my sweater and made me stop. Then he started barking and bouncing till I followed him in the opposite direction. It was lucky I did, as I found out there was another path I had not seen. Teo went ahead along the path and we soon found Mum and Dad, who had just realized I'd disappeared and were out of their minds.

I think Teo saved my life today.

I ran and ran down the slopes and up the slopes, and every now and then I ran back to the others to see if all was well. It was lucky I did as, during one of my inspections, I saw that Tommy had disappeared. He was nowhere to be seen but Marianna and Corrado didn't seem to mind, engaged as they were shouting at the top of their voices.

Where the heck has Tommy gone? I wondered and I ran back as fast as I could. It was such a relief when I found him crouched behind a bush doing pooh!

I waited till he'd finished and then we started going. Tommy ran in front of me and I soon realized he was going the wrong way.

The problem with Tommy is that he doesn't stop and smell things like I do. That's why he gets into all sorts of trouble! If he could only sniff things, he'd know exactly where to go.

Anyway, I managed to make him understand he was on the wrong track so we turned and went the right way.

We soon found Mum and Dad, who went crazy the moment we came in sight. "Where have you been? We've been calling you for hours! Stop sticking to that silly dog all the time! Leave him alone! Let him get lost!"

GET LOST to me?!? "GET LOST TO ME after ALL THAT I HAD DONE?!?

Tommy STICKING to ME?

What would have happened had I not been STICKING TO HIM?

How mean of them! How ungrateful!

We're

home at last. It's almost dark and I'm dead tired but I'm not going to do without a little match before dinner. No way!

As I get out of the car, the first thing I see is aunt Camilla wandering near the fence. She's peering into the bushes and wriggling her hands. She's calling: "Giselle! Giselle!" and she looks as if she was coming apart from the seams.

" What's the matter?" I wonder aloud as I walk up to her.

As soon as she sees me she cries: "Oh, it's you! Tommy, isn't it? You know my niece Giselle, don't you? She said you've become good friends."

"Well, yes... I mean..."

"I can't find her anywhere now! Have you seen her?"

"No. Actually, we've just ..."

"What's the matter?" Dad asks.

"My niece Giselle!" This time our neighbour almost
cries. "She should be at home watching TV, but she's not!
I've looked everywhere! Even in the garden, even though I
made her promise she would stay inside.   Where can she
have gone, I wonder... She doesn't know anyone here,
apart from your son. What could have happened to her? I
keep calling and calling... I've almost lost my voice. Why
doesn't she hear me? And it's getting dark! I wanted her
to come with me to the charity fair, but she wouldn't. I
shouldn't have gone without her! I shouldn't have left her
all alone. And now I don't know where she is. I don't know
what may have happened to her. What can I do now?
She's such a difficult girl to get along with... and I don't

really know what to do... I have no experience with children, you know..."

And so on and so forth, talking at a mile a minute. Now I know what aunt Camilla and Giselle have in common!

At last Dad interrupts her. "You shouldn't worry so much. You'll see she'll turn up at any moment."

And Mum, who's just joined us, says: "Have you looked in her bedroom? She may be listening to music, her earphones on. You know what youngsters are like."

Our neighbour looks outraged. "Of course I looked in her bedroom! She's not there, believe me!" Then she shakes her head and takes a big sigh. "The problem is that I have no experience with children and Giselle is a bit out of herself. You know... her granny, I mean, my mother... well, she recently died and..."

"Oh, I'm so sorry to hear that!" Mum screams. "When did this happen?"

"Twenty days ago."

"Twenty days? But that's such a short time ago!" Mum looks shocked now.

"And has your niece come here for the holidays?" Dad asks.

"Actually, she's come to stay! I'm her aunt on her mother's side and her only family left. She lost her parents when she was only eight, poor girl. That was very hard on her..."

"Oh, dear me!" Mum cries out again, interrupting her. "How did it happen?"

"A car accident."

"And how old is your niece now?" Dad asks.

"Eleven."

"So was she brought up by her grandmother? I mean, your mother?" Dad says.

Aunt Camilla just nods. She's still looking around as if she expected to see her niece spring up out of nowhere.

I think I know where Giselle is. I walk a few steps away

looking for Teo.

Funny! I can't see him anywhere. The evening light is rapidly turning into darkness and it's blurring the shapes of things. "Teo!" I call. A small shuffling noise comes from inside the car. Good grief! He's still in the boot!

I rush to the car. When I open the boot, Teo sits up, scratches hard behind his ear and then flops down again without even opening his eyes.

"Come on, Teo, get out!" I say. Teo shoots a drowsy glance at me without moving his head.

I tell him to move on again, but he doesn't stir. In the end, I have to drag him out.

As soon as he's on the ground, he shakes himself all over and then he shuffles miserably off towards the fence, his tail sagging. He looks as if he was going to drop asleep any moment.

I follow him and whisper in his ear. "Go and look for Giselle in the den."

My command only draws a blank stare.

"Go and look for Giselle. Go!" I hiss.

W_{hat}

the heck! I know exactly what Tommy wants me to do, but all I can think about is sleeping after running all day. Unfortunately, Tommy means what he says and I have no choice.

I start moving towards the tunnel. When I get to the entrance I look around to make sure nobody can see me, then I slip in and I crawl to the Den. Giselle is there. She's sleeping, but as soon as I lick her face, she startles and springs up, eyes wide open. "Oh, it's you!" she says. "You gave me such a fright! Thanks a lot for waking me up!"

Then she kisses me on the nose and crawls away.

I get out of the tunnel on my side of the fence and I can hear her voice on the other side. She's calling her aunt.

Giselle

has popped out from nowhere and aunt Camilla almost faints with relief. Then she starts close questioning her in our presence and she can't seem to be able to stop. Where were you, what were you doing, why didn't you answer me, why weren't you where I thought you should have been... and so on and so forth.

Even a saint would have lost their temper! Personally, I

wouldn't have been able to stand her!

But Giselle is very patient and tells all sorts of lies, speaking calmly all the time, a little smile on her face.

She says she was in the house... she was reading a book in the attic... she hadn't answered because she hadn't heard her aunt come in... she'd been waiting for her all the time... she was so sorry she hadn't heard her calling...

Why in the attic? Aunt Camilla asks. But then she shuts up as she had not actually thought of looking in the attic.

Then she thanks us a real lot for our help, for our patience, for talking to her in a moment of distress and so on and so forth. Giselle keeps glancing sheepishly at me the whole time and I think she's right when she says that her aunt is a real nag.

In the end, we manage to get away from aunt Camilla and I can switch on the computer at last.

I might still have the time for a match before dinner.

A_{nd} what about me? I only hope they don't think the little bit of bread and salami they gave me was enough for the rest of the day! I'm starving!

And the biscuit? Will they give me a biscuit tonight?

I DESERVE A BISCUIT!

I don't want to sound a boaster but I think I can safely say I rescued both Tommy and Giselle today.

If it hadn't been for me, what would have happened to them?

But who knows what I did? NO-ONE KNOWS. NO-ONE CARES.

And a THANK-YOU? Has anyone thanked me?

And WHAT ABOUT MY SUPPER? I'm afraid they're going to forget my supper, poor me!

And WHAT ABOUT MY BISCUIT?

If they don't even give me a biscuit, tonight, I'll have to dig up some of those bones...

Rats

The castle is infested by huge rats which spring out from everywhere and try to bite the king and the queen, the maids of honour, the king's counsellors, the prince, the princess, the knights, the jester... I shoot at all the rats I see, but some slither away getting out of the tapestry, the carpet, the torches on the wall... even the teapot spout, the chimney... It's pretty hard to catch them all.

All the rats must be killed before they get to bite the characters as anyone who's bitten is cloned. This means that another character looking exactly like the first turns up. There's only a tiny difference, which can hardly be detected at first sight.

Right now, the princess has been bitten on her shoulder and another princess immediately springs up, apparently identical to the first, but with a light blue star on her forehead. Luckily, I've been able to spot the difference before the double disappears from the screen so, when one of the two princesses appears again, I'll know whether I must go on protecting her from the rats or leave her to her destiny if she's a clone.

There are 3,000 rats. I win 1,000 points for one hundred killings and lose 200 points every time a character is bitten. I get a bonus of 1,000 points when I reach 3,000 and one every 500 more. I win the game at 10,000 points.

I'm still at 2,500.

Look at that! A rat is slithering out of the jester's sleeve! I shoot and miss. Oh, bother! The rat's bitten the jester! Now I need to spot the difference in the double before it disappears. "I got it!" I shout. Yellow and orange striped trousers, no longer yellow and orange spotted ones.

The rhythm of the game is getting quicker. Not even one thousand eyes could keep the situation under control. Then I suddenly feel Dad's hand on my shoulder. I startle and miss three rats. One of these bites the knight. "Is this a new game? I don't remember seeing it before." Dad says.

I get goose pimples all over, but then I brace up and manage to say: "Oh, it's an old game, actually! From last year, you know..."

I see the knight's double has two swords hanging from his belt. That was easy, but Dad's hand is still splayed on my shoulder.

"Hmm... I think I'm through..." I say trying to shoot a rat

that's just come out of a maid's shoe. "I'm fed up."

"Good idea." Dad says, his hand still on my shoulder.

Good grief, why doesn't he leave me alone?

"Yes, a very good idea." I hear Mum say at my back.

Oh, heck! Mum too! That's just what I needed!

 "You'd better go and have a shower so you'll be ready for bed after dinner. You must be pretty tired after today's hike." Mum says.

"I'm not that tired, actually."

Oh, bother! The game is getting out of control! Far too many rats are running about undisturbed. Luckily the phone rings. Mum goes to answer. One less in the way! But Dad is still lingering nearby. I try to regain ground shooting to the full, vaguely aware of the formal tone in Mum's voice as she answers the phone. "Yes, it's me. Good-evening! How are you?"

Then she falls into silence and when she starts talking again, there's a hint of stiffness in her voice: "Hold on a minute, will you? I'm going to call my husband. I think you'd better talk to him, if you don't mind."

I can't help glancing at her, even though this means missing loads of rats.

She glances back, covers the receiver and yells: "Tommy!!! Are you still there? I thought I told you to go and have a shower! I meant: AT ONCE!"

A full dozen rats swarm everywhere. The game is totally spoiled now. It's no use trying to keep it going. I grumble a bit but switch off. A moment later, as I'm climbing the stairs, I overhear Mum say: "It's Tommy's coach."

I stop dead. THE COACH? Why? How's that?

"What does he want?" Dad asks.

"You'd better come and talk to him yourself."

I sit down slowly on one of the steps, my heart thumping.

I hear Dad say: "Hallo. This is Corrado Aladino, Tommy's

father... good-evening... Yes, of course, what's up?"

It takes ages before Dad says anything else. When he speaks again his voice is somewhat icy. "Excuse me, but I don't think we should discuss this on the phone. I'd rather talk to you in person. What if I came over at the next training session? ... I see... Right. Well, we'll do as you say then. So that would be... tomorrow at lunch break? Fine! And where can we meet? ... OK, that's fine with me. I'll be there. Goodnight!"

As I hear the click of the phone being hung up, I stand up and sneak upstairs, my legs shaking. I wonder what's going on. Could it be something connected with The Two? I feel paralysed with fear.

I get under the shower. The jet of water on my head reminds me of yesterday's rain.

I was sitting on the bench, the rain drumming on the hood of my KW, its thin needles piercing my head. The Two, who had turned up in the middle of the second half, were sitting behind me. Even though I didn't look at them, I felt their piercing glares on my back. I just couldn't stand it, so I got to my feet and went to ask the coach if I could go to the changing rooms. He glared at me for a moment but then he gave me the key without saying a word.

I immediately headed for the changing rooms and out of the corner of one eye I saw that The Two were following me. As soon as we got into the thicket I stopped and took the fifty Euros out of my pocket. When The Two approached, I handed the money without looking up.

"That's a clever ass-hole!" sneered the fair headed guy with his bored, drawling voice, coming closer and closer until we were almost nose to nose. "But don't forget next Tuesday! That will make fifty more."

I didn't say a word and started to back away.

"Oh, are you already going away, you nitwit? Why are you in such a hurry? Why not stay here for a nice little chat? Oh, I see... going back to the match, are you? See how everyone's waiting for you..."

"Yes, just to give you a kick in the ass!" cried out the short nerd as he burst out laughing. Drops of rain were dripping from his red crest. Now the fair-haired nerd was also roaring with laughter.

I just couldn't stand all this any longer, so I spun round and took flight, but after a few steps I slipped and fell flat on my face. I got back to my feet as fast as I could and ran away followed by loud guffaws, a taste of slimy earth in my mouth and a stinging pain in my eyes.

When I got to the changing rooms the door was ajar, so I got in without using the key. My own face bounced back at me from the reflection in the large mirror on the opposite wall. It made me startle as it was almost totally covered in mud. I realized I must have been crying, as two pale streaks were running down my cheeks.

I knew The Two had not followed me but I locked the

door all the same and then I went to wash my face in the basin. I filled my mouth with warm water, over and over again, but I couldn't send away the nasty taste of grainy stuff in my mouth. I also tried to wash my arms, my KW, my shorts, my legs and even my shoes. A vain effort, especially on the clothes, which now showed large brownish spots all over.

Eventually, I thought I heard the click of the door handle being turned, as if someone was trying to get in, but when I looked nothing stirred.

When I got back to the football ground at last, the game was over and as soon as the coach saw me he yelled: "What happened? I thought you were never going to come back!"

"I was sick." I said.

"Again!" he snapped, looking at my dirty clothes and then at the key I had just put in his hands. "Did you lock the door?"

"Of course, I did."

"Dinner's ready!"

This was Mum calling from downstairs.

I get out of the shower. I wonder what they're going to tell me now. I dry myself and then put on my pyjamas. I've decided not to go down for dinner. I'll just talk to them from the top of the stairs. I'll say I have a stomach ache and I don't feel like eating anything. That's a pity though, as I'm starving in spite of it all, but...

"Tommy, aren't you coming?"

Dad's voice startles me. I hadn't heard him come up. I peer into his eyes. I'm dying to know what the coach told him but I don't dare ask... also because I'm not supposed to have been listening. Anyway, Dad doesn't look particularly angry or upset, only a bit tired, I decide, so I probably have no reason to worry.

"I'm coming! I'm starving." I say, heading for the door.

"Good!" Dad says, a faint smile on his face. "And then

straight to bed."

Mum is already sitting at the table. She doesn't look particularly concerned. So I gulp my soup down and when I've finished I ask for more.

"I see you were starving." Dad says filling my plate. "By the way, that video-game you were playing at... you know... I don't remember seeing it before..."

I blush furiously and the soup gets stuck in my mouth. I find nothing better to do but feign a coughing fit. Then, when I recover, I try to speak in an even voice. "I already told you it's an old one! I've had it for years..."

"I thought you said we bought it last year."

"Well, I don't actually remember. It's quite old anyway..."

"I see. I was wondering, you'd ask me for the money to buy a new video-game if you wanted one, wouldn't you?"

"Of course, I would!" I keep silent for a moment and then I say: "But you wouldn't buy me a new video-game, would you?"

"I would! Obviously you'd have to do some chores as a way of compensation, like for example..."

"I know." I interrupt him. "Can I go to bed now?" I ask, pushing my plate away.

"Aren't you going to finish your soup?" Mum asks.

"I'm not hungry any more."

"Fine! It'll go to the dog, then. He'll be happy. Take your plate to the kitchen before going up."

A few minutes later, as I slip into bed, I think to myself that I can't possibly go on like this. I wonder why the coach phoned, what he told Dad, why he wants to see him tomorrow, why Dad did not say anything about this, why he asked me about the video-game... I can't go on like this, I NEED TO ACT, I must. I thrust my head under the pillow and I suddenly know what I'll do. First thing tomorrow morning I'll put a note in the fence. I only hope Giselle sees it.

CHAPTER FIVE

(Monday, 18th July)

Collecting the Dew

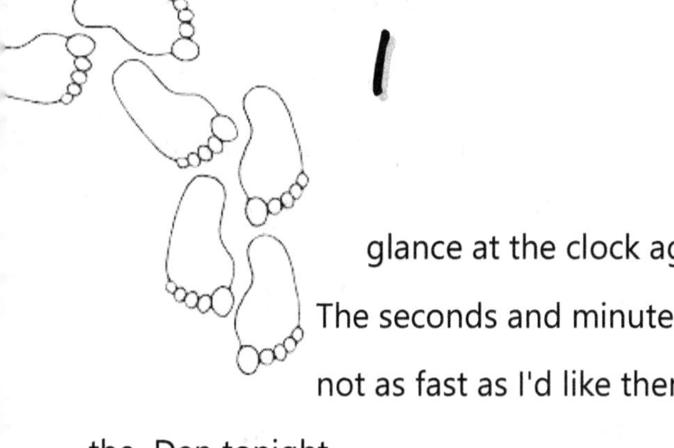

I glance at the clock again and again. The seconds and minutes speed by, but not as fast as I'd like them to. I'm going to the Den tonight.

I don't think this is the best thing I can do, actually, but it is the only idea I have, even though I racked my brains for hours to find a different solution.

In the note to Giselle I said I would be there at 11.30, but I've been ready since about 9.30. I'm wearing a tracksuit on top of my pyjamas, tennis shoes and a miner's torch around the head. I've pulled the blanket up so that it covers my face and every now and then I switch on the torch to make sure it works. My old school diary is in my trouser pocket and it is poking at my hip every time I turn. I also have a pen inside my top pocket.

What time is it? Eleven twenty and fifteen seconds...

I can hear Dad's intermittent snoring from the main bedroom. This means he's sleeping, of course, but I can't tell about Mum, unfortunately, as she doesn't snore.

What time is it? Eleven twenty-one minutes and two seconds... Time to go.

I feel nervous, I admit. Getting out in the middle of the night is not something I like doing. Anyway, Teo should be there waiting.

I slip out of bed trying not to make the slightest noise

and I tiptoe downstairs peering in the dark. I creep across the hall holding my breath, I get to the front door, unlock it and I'm out. Phew!

There's no trace of Teo, though. Where has he gone?

Luckily it's not as dark as I thought, even though the moon is now hiding behind a cloud. Shredded clouds are sweeping the sky now, so moonlight comes and goes.

I start walking, keeping close to the side wall of the house, and when it ends I start running as fast as I can. I run through the orchard and out of the corner of my eye I see furtive shadows moving at my sides, but they swiftly disappear when I turn my head. The sudden hoot of an owl sends me running even faster. When I finally get to the thicket near the fence, I take a few deep breaths to calm down, then I duck and peer into the bushes. Where's the entrance to the tunnel? I can't see it! There are only thick clusters of brambles in front of me.

Fear clutches my stomach now. I want to go back to

bed. I can't get into these bushes in this horrible darkness. I absolutely can't.

I turn on my heels and start walking back toward the house, then my heart gives a horrible jolt as I feel a grab at my trousers. I spin around and I see it's Teo. I take a deep breath and I shout at him: "You gave me such a fright, you mongrel!" Teo sits and bends his head, glancing up at me warily from under his knitted eyebrows.

"OK, never mind." I say. "Is Giselle there?"

Teo springs up and goes to the bushes. Then he turns to see if I am following him. I take a deep sigh. "OK. Let me see where the hole is." Teo gets into the bushes. I get on my fours and start crawling behind him.

The tunnel is stifling. My torch lightens only a small spot at a time and leaves the rest in total darkness. I feel an icy chill running through my spine as I think I can hear breathing and whispers all around. Anything might be hiding here! Tears spring into my eyes and I angrily rub them away with the back of my hand. At last we get to the den.

I start breathing again only when I see Giselle sitting on a blanket in the middle of a faint spot of light. She's hugging her knees and she breaks into a smile as soon as she sees me.

I sit down next to her without saying a word, I don't trust my voice yet. Teo comes and sits between us. Pitch darkness hovers all around the small circle of light of Giselle's torch and I feel like being enclosed inside solid, stifling black walls. I take a deep breath and then I force my face into a smile.

"Want one?" Giselle asks pulling out a box of biscuits from under her sweater.

I slip a hand inside the box and take a biscuit.

"Where did you go yesterday?"

"Hiking in the mountain. " I say, munching.

"Did you see what a fuss aunt Camilla made?"

"Yes, I know... a real nag, isn't she?"

"Luckily Teodorico woke me up just in time. It would have been tragic if he hadn't."

"Actually, I sent him to you, you know. I saw your aunt was having convulsions. I thought you had to be here... What were you doing?"

"Just waiting. But then I fell asleep."

"Waiting for me?"

"Yes, I had nothing else to do and I thought you might turn up sooner or later."

We fall silent again. I take another biscuit from the box and put it in my mouth.

"I'll show you my book now." Giselle says, pulling out an old, small, funny handbag in rigid brown leather all cracked and smelling of mildew from under her sweater.

Teo reaches out and smells it carefully.

"What's this?"

"The book I told you about is inside this bag."

"Oh, I see..."

She pulls hard at the metal frame to unclasp the bag and then she takes a small book with a wizened leather cover out of it. The book is bound with a pink ribbon, which Giselle unfastens. Then she places the book on the stone near the torch and opens it carefully. I see that there are many loose pages. The sheets are yellowish and there are plenty of brownish spots along the edges.

"It's not brand new, is it?"

"It's very old, actually. It dates back to the beginning of the twentieth century."

"That old?" I say putting another biscuit in my mouth.

"It's a present from my Granny..." she says with a tinge of sadness in her voice. "She got it from her mother."

"Oh, I see." I lean forward to read the title on the cover: The words **"Magic Spells"** pop up and start dancing under my eyes. I suddenly feel sick. I shake my head repeatedly. "I don't think this can be of any help." I say.

"Don't make a fuss!" Giselle snaps "We only need to look for the right spell."

I plunge my hand into the biscuits box, pull out three biscuits and put them all in my mouth.

Teo licks his lips, sighs and stares at me imploringly.

I hand him a biscuit. Teo swallows it whole, without even tasting it. Then he opens his mouth and sticks out his tongue, a large grin on his face and slobber dripping everywhere.

"OK, just one more, but this will be the last." I say.

Teo swallows the second biscuit. Then he puts his head down on his legs with a big sigh.

"He knows you're not going to give him any more." Giselle says. She sounds awed. "He understands every single word."

Teo lifts his head and sticks out his tongue in a broad smile.

"I don't think so." I say. "I think he just heard us say his name."

Teo puts his tongue back, places his head on his legs and sighs.

I yawn. "So, what are we going to do now?"

"I just told you. We need to find the right spell."

Giselle starts turning the pages gingerly. Then she stops. "I was forgetting that we need to read the prologue first of all."

"What's a prologue?"

"It's preliminary information on the book as a whole."

"I see..."

I'm not sure I know what "preliminary" exactly means, but I don't feel like telling her.

"Do you want me to read it for you?" Giselle asks eagerly.

"What?"

Giselle rolls her eyes. "The prologue."

"Yes, why not?"

I suspect this preliminary prologue must be awfully boring. Anyway, as I've come here, I can't be too choosy. I put one more biscuit in my mouth.

Giselle reads: "Before endeavouring to elaborate the sundry topics at stake, we shall inevitably have to insist on a fundamental notion..."

I can't help yawning again.

"You're falling asleep!" Giselle snaps, shaking my arm.

"I'm not!" I retort "but I couldn't understand a word."

Giselle sighs. "I know. The language is pretty strange... I also had problems understanding it the first time. You know what? I'm going to tell you what it says in plain words."

"OK"

"Well... The prologue basically says that a spell works only if you try really hard to make it work."

"What does that mean?"

"That you can't just cast the spell and wait. You also have to do your best to achieve your aim."

"Do my best… at what?"

"Oh, dear! Don't you understand?"

I just shake my head. I don't dare say anything else. I feel stupid.

"It says you have to find a way to make things happen."

"So, in other words, I cast the spell and then I behave as if I hadn't done it, right?"

"Well… in a way it's like you said, but…"

"That means your magic spell isn't good for me."

Giselle raises her eyes to heaven and sighs. In the faint light of the torch her hair has a golden gleam but her eyes, so clear in daylight, now seem to be as dark and deep as the bottom of a well. A shiver runs down my spine.

"You said you wanted to learn how to play soccer, didn't you?"

Her tone of voice tells me that she might lose her temper very soon but I am determined to speak my mind. "I did, but... honestly, I don't think this booklet can be of any help."

"How can you say that if you don't try it first?" Giselle snaps. Anyway, you're not going to find a spell on soccer here..."

"So, you see I'm right!"

"But there are a lot of other intents! Plenty of them! You'll just have to find the one that fits best."

I keep quiet trying hard to concentrate on the possible meaning of the word "intents". Then I pick up another biscuit from the box and start munching noisily.

"Why don't you read the intents yourself?" Giselle suggests, pushing the book towards me. "You may find something that is just right for you."

I start leafing the pages and I finally understand what intents are. They're just the titles. There's a different title at the top of each page and under each title there's some writing... in rhyme. WHAT? Are these poems? I can't believe it! POEMS!

I lean down to read the titles in the dim light and I flush purple. WHAT STUFF IS THIS?

How to gain the heart of your beloved.

How to make your beloved appear in your dreams.

How to transform friendship into love.

"What stuff is this? " I snap, pushing the book back towards Giselle.

Giselle pushes it back towards me. "Come on! Keep reading! You'll see you'll find the right spell sooner or later!"

I go back to the book with a snort.

The fourth title... well, this is quite different, actually:

How to keep a cool head when you are in danger and find the courage to fight against adversities ... the fifth... *How to take your revenge for wrongs you have suffered* ... the sixth...

I stop because I suddenly come up with an idea. The last two intents might be right for me!

Actually, the first sounds particularly interesting. If I got the meaning right, it should tell me how to pick up enough courage to fight against The Two, as they actually are a sort of adversity, aren't they? I'd like to be able to fight against them rather than run away as I always do. I wouldn't mind taking my revenge, of course, but that can wait. The first thing I need is courage.

"I have it!" I declare. Number four is exactly what I need!"

Giselle leans down to read, then she frowns and

gawks at me. "Danger? Adversities? I don't see how this can be connected with soccer. " she says.

"It does, believe me."

"In what way?"

Giselle keeps staring at me and I fight hard to hold her gaze. "I know what I'm saying. If I keep a cool head when I play soccer I'll probably be able to play better, don't you think so?"

Giselle shakes her head. "I don't think you got the meaning right!"

"I did." I insist, swallowing one more biscuit.

Giselle shrugs. "OK, then. Now, let's see what the book says. Do you want me to go on reading it for you?"

I don't answer and put one more biscuit in my mouth. Giselle takes this as a yes and starts reading.

Intent Number Four

How to keep a cool head when you are in

danger and find the courage to fight against adversities.

Prologue

"Take heed of my words if you have it in your heart to...

I snort. "Listen, we'd better stop it here."

"But we've hardly started!" Giselle cries.

"I know... but you see... the fact is that I don't understand a single word of what you're reading! What does 'take heed' mean?"

"OK, I'll read the text first and then I'll tell you what it says."

I shrug and take a deep sigh of resignation. "Right, then! Do as you like."

Giselle starts reading to herself and I keep silent. Even though she's a bit nuts, I think she's really trying to help me.

At last she says: "I think I know what it means. It means that if you want to get out of trouble, you must mainly rely on your courage and determination. Do you want me to go on?"

"OK. Keep going."

"Now I'll read the spell. Where's your pen? You'd better take notes or you won't remember. You need to be very accurate and follow the instructions scrupulously when you cast a spell, otherwise it may not work."

"Take notes?"

"Yes, I told you, didn't I?"

The tone in her voice makes me understand that I'd better not contradict her, so I take out my diary and pen without daring to say one more word.

Giselle starts reading, her voice drawling in the air like a lullaby.

Part One

Rise early in the morning
when the sky is light blue
the lark is singing
and the sun is new.
Wet your brow with the dew
you 'll collect from the grass
repeating ten times
"Another day will not pass
before my wish comes true."

Part Two

Put a pinch of salt
on the tip of your tongue
shut your eyes to daylight
clench your teeth
and fists tight

then ten times say aloud:
"To myself I swear
adversities will no more
make my head so sore
as against them I shall fight
to the best of my might."

Part Three

Put odd socks on your feet
wear underpants inside out
draw a circle around you
while you sit on the ground.
Then repeat to yourself:
"Whatever happens to me,
back here I'll be bound
and inside this circle
I'll be safe and sound."

It takes a while before I realize Giselle has stopped reading and is now staring at me with burning eyes.

"It sounds rather complicated..." I say, shaking the box to see whether there are any biscuits left. A few crumbs fall down on the blanket and Teo promptly licks them away. Then he grabs the box between his teeth and starts munching at it.

"It's not that difficult if you have your list." Giselle retorts. "Did you put everything down? What did you write?"

I cast a quick glance at my diary and read: "Collect the dew..."

"And then?"

"Just, collect the dew. That's it."

"Nothing else?"

"You were reading too fast..."

Giselle rolls her eyes and then she says: "OK. Never mind! Just write what I say."

Dictation goes on for a while and in the end I have a list of silly things I ought to do if I want to cast the spell. Nothing could be more stupid!

I read the list over and over again trying to make sense out of it, but I keep telling myself I'll never do things such as getting up at dawn, picking up the dew from the lawn, putting salt on my tongue, wearing odd socks and inside-out underpants... Above all, I'll never, never say all those stupid, soppy, screwy things!

"Fine! I'm sure it'll work." I say, as I snap my diary shut and put it back into my pocket.

Giselle doesn't answer and I'm suddenly aware of the deep silence all around us. For a moment I believe that a spell has been really cast upon us. Then Teo starts snoring, his head firmly placed on the tattered box.

"I'm sure this is going to work." I repeat, just to say something.

Giselle rolls her eyes. "Come on! I know you don't trust

the spell... and you didn't tell the truth when you said you wanted to learn how to play soccer, did you?"

I shrug. "Well, actually, there's also something else on my mind." I admit.

"And you don't want to tell me what this something else is, do you?"

I keep silent and stare at the ground.

Giselle shrugs. "Well, never mind!" she says.

"Anyway..."

"Never mind!" she repeats.

Giselle stops talking and I start thinking. What I'd really like to tell her now is how sorry I am about her Granny being dead, and her parents being dead, too, but the only words that come out of my mouth are: "Thank you, anyway."

"My pleasure. I've got to go now." she says.

Giselle binds the book with the pink ribbon and puts it back into the bag. She thrusts the bag under her sweater and stands up. I stand up, too, and together we fold the blanket. After that she puts the blanket around her shoulders and crawls away, the torch in her mouth.

"Shall I see you tomorrow?" I call after her, but she doesn't answer. I shrug. I suddenly become aware of a strange noise all around me.

How funny! Everything was so deadly silent a minute ago and now there's such a shuffling... rubbing noise... such insistent whispering everywhere.

 Cold shivers of fear run down my spine as I wonder what may be going on. I frenziedly put the torch around my head.

"Let's go to bed, Teo. I'm dead tired." I say, trying to keep my voice even.

Teo opens his eyes and jumps up, grabs the tattered box in his mouth and disappears into the tunnel. I follow him closely.   I want to get away from this horrible place as soon as I can.

CHAPTER SIX

(Tuesday, 19th July)

Thunder and Lightning

The

sky was pitch dark when Teo and I got out of the tunnel last night. Heavy clouds had covered the moon and a strong wind was shaking the tree branches. Teo and I rushed towards home. Suddenly, a streak of lightning crossed the sky and, in the sudden glare, the old olive tree jumped at us, its twisted branches widely spread like the open arms of a ghost.

We got into the house just as the thunder came, its

rumble luckily covering the noise of the front door banging shut and of our leaps up the stairs. As soon as I stepped into my bedroom I kicked off my shoes and slipped into bed without taking my clothes off. Teo hid under the bed.

Teo is afraid of thunderstorms.

I pulled the covers over my head. Through the loose weave of the summer blanket I could still see the glare of lightning and I started measuring the interval of time between the glare and the rumble. First I counted up to ten and reckoned the storm must be 70 kilometres away, then up to seven... so that was 49 kilometres, then six, then three... three was only 21 kilometres away! The thunderstorm was getting nearer.

While I was wondering if seven was the right number for this kind of reckoning or if it was just the multiplier we use when comparing the age of dogs to that of people, a blinding streak of lightning, a deafening rumble of thunder and a tremendous downpour of rain fell down on the roof over our heads almost at the same time. I heard Teo whimper from under the bed and I felt cold shivers run down my spine as I thought I could still be there, under those bushes...

I would have risked my life... what for? Just for that silly, sloppy, screwy nonsense that Giselle calls MAGIC SPELLS!

How stupid of me just to sit there and listen to that mass of ridiculous tales in sloppy verse!

And how stupid of me to think I would be able to settle things right in this silly way!

How stupid of me!

How so VERY, VERY STUPID OF ME!!!

I kept tossing and turning for a long time before I fell asleep. This morning I woke up to a gentle beating of rain on the window panes. The rumble of thunder could still be heard in the distance and the lightning had become a faint, intermittent glare.

Teo had come up from under the bed and he was sound asleep on my feet.

I got to sleep again, too, and when I woke up, the room was lit by the sun and Teo was sleeping close to me, his head on my pillow. I hugged him and kissed him on the nose. Teo yawned and purred like a cat.

Then I heard the noise of steps coming up the stairs. I leaped out and tried to pull Teo away, hoping to have the time to hide him under the bed. But he had just started to stir when Mum got in.

I'll never forget the shocked look of disbelief on her face when she saw the two of us, me standing in my socks and sweat-suit and Teo innocently looking up at her from my bed, his ears cocked and his front legs splayed on my pillow.

It was the matter of an instant before she thundered: "What's the dog doing here?"

I tried to explain that I had put Teo in because he was

afraid of the storm, that I was wearing my sweat-suit and

socks because I had been cold, that Teo had spent the

night under the bed and had jumped on it only when he'd

heard her steps on the stairs...

But there was nothing to do. She wouldn't believe me.

She said that even if Teo had been afraid of the

thunderstorm, that was not a good reason for letting him

in, not to mention letting him stay on my bed! And on

my pillow! Really!!! That, if it was absolutely necessary, he

would have to be put in the cupboard, that he had his

shed out in the garden, anyway, that I should have

woken her up before venturing out in the storm... and

what a shock for her all that was! She would never have

thought of having to see something like that in all her life!

And we could not even imagine how many germs,

bacteria, fleas, viruses, ticks the dog must have shed on my

sheets and, even worse, on my pillow! That she would

have to change the sheets and wash the blankets and

hoover the mattress and wash the floor with bleach... and

the smell!!! What about that foul smell? How long would it take before it faded out?

Mum kept talking for minutes on end until Teo, after a time of total petrification, finally leapt out of the bed and went to hide beneath it.

"Get him out!" Mum thundered again. "At once!"

I bent down and stretched out my arm under the bed but Teo had flattened himself against the wall on the other side and I just couldn't reach him.

Seeing that, Mum thundered: "I'm going now and you put the dog out at once! And take a shower before you come down for breakfast! And when you are in the shower check that there aren't any ticks sticking to your skin. Is that clear?"

I nodded repeatedly. Sometimes Mum gives me the creeps. When she is in one of her moods I don't dare breathe. The only thing I can do is keep silent and do as she says.

On Second Thoughts

When

I finally sat down for breakfast Mum's fit of anger had turned into a resounding grumble, punctuated by a long series of exclamation marks. "That's just what I needed! Ha! A dog in the house! As if I didn't have enough to do! I'm sick and tired of all this!" and so on and so forth.

It's taken time, but now she's stopped grumbling at last, and I can start thinking my own thoughts.

I look at the shining puddles along the driveway and I wonder where I may have put my rubber boots, but then Mum suddenly declares: "It's high time you started doing your summer homework."

SUMMER HOMEWORK?

I'm taken aback. For a moment I can't even understand what "summer homework" actually means. "Well…" I then say "I don't really have that much to do!"

"Whatever you have to do, you must start doing it right now! The sooner the better! I won't have any of those bad marks next year!"

Considering what has just happened, I don't dare contradict her and ten minutes later I'm scowling at a thick schoolbook I've placed on the living room table. It's our literature textbook. I've hidden my old diary beneath it and I've put a few comics beneath the diary. Then I sit, I open the book at random and start thinking my own thoughts again.

The first thing I think is that it's a pity having to sit here doing nothing while I might go out in the sun or play one of my video-games. My eyes wander from the computer to the window, and back to the computer.

I can see Teo through the window, in the garden. He looks fast asleep, as usual. But I know for sure that he's not really sleeping, he's only pretending to. Actually, he's waiting. He's waiting for me to get out of the house.

I know how he feels and I agree with him. Sleeping, or pretending to sleep, is such an easy way to while the time away...

I put my head on my arms and close my eyes but a shuffling noise tells me Mum is coming by, so I steady up at once and I start performing "the perfect student" show: my elbows on the table, my hands cupped around my chin to sustain the weight of my very heavy head, my eyes half closed and a weary murmur steadily coming out of my mouth. Now and then, a deep sigh shows how hard I'm working and how deadly tired I am.

Mum falls hands and feet in the trap and she asks me: "What are you studying?"

"Oh... nothing...!" I say.

I have no idea, actually. I try to gain time by giving a quick look at the page I opened at random. "I'm just … I'm… revising a poem."

"A poem?"

"A poem we read in class. It's a poem by… by a poet who's called… Frost."

"I see. And what's the poem about?"

I glance at the page and the first word that strikes me is woods. "It's about woods." I say

"Woods?" Mum stares at me blankly. Luckily, she seems to have lost interest and, after a few moments, she shuffles upstairs.

I look at the page again and I read the final lines of the poem.

The woods are lovely, dark, and deep,
But I have promises to keep,
And miles to go before I sleep,
And miles to go before I sleep.

I always read the final lines of poems only. In my opinion, all we need to know about a poem is what the poet writes at the end of it. Funnily enough, I think I know what the poet means. Like the poet, I also feel as if I had miles to go. I pull the diary from under the schoolbook and I start reading the notes I took last night.

I know they are a heap of nonsense but now I'm no longer sure I don't want to try the spell.

What would be the risk if I did? At worst the spell will not work. Anyway, why not give it a chance?

As I start reading, I begin to think that casting a spell may not be so difficult as I thought.

Getting up at dawn would be pretty hard, I admit, as I'm a late sleeper, but I would do it if I really had to... and it would take nothing to dip my fingers in the grass and wet my forehead with the dew. Then I would have to repeat those stupid lines aloud but that, again, would not be a problem. I would only have to make sure no-one is listening.

What else? Well, putting a tip of salt on the tip of my tongue would not be a problem either... apart from the fact that it doesn't say if it should be kitchen or table salt...

And what about sitting on the floor? Actually, here it says ground, not floor... so, where should I sit? Would it have to be in the open? On the grass? Would I have to go to the Den and sit there?

I don't think so... I suppose my bedroom floor would do.

Anyway, what would I have to draw a circle with? Would it have to be a real circle or an imaginary one? If it should be real I would need a piece of chalk; for an imaginary circle I might use a stick instead.

Wearing odd socks might be a problem. What if Mum sees them? Besides it doesn't say how long I should keep them on. The whole day? As long as it is necessary? If the spell must be repeated over and over again and as long as the problem lasts, I'm afraid I'll have to wear odd socks and inside-out underpants for the rest of the summer!

I go on thinking about the spell for quite a long time and all this thinking makes me feel awfully sleepy, so I put my head down on my arms and I close my eyes.

Suddenly, the shuffle comes dangerously near again so I promptly steady up, slip the diary back underneath the schoolbook and start mumbling to myself.

Then the shuffle goes away and I put my head down on my arms again, thinking.

"Tommy!!! Really!!! I can't believe it! You're sleeping!"

I open one eye and see Mum towering over me, hands on her hips.

"I'm not sleeping at all!" I scream, outraged. "I have miles to go before I sleep!"

Running Around The Tree

The

sky's so clear I can easily see the darker patches on the moon.

I'm sitting in front of the window, waiting for the biscuit, as usual, but tonight I feel there's a threat in the air, something that makes my ears prick and lifts the fur on my back. From time to time a grumbling sound comes out of my throat and my legs are so restless that I can't keep still.

So I decide to go for a run around the olive tree.

I run and run around the tree, then I go back to the

window and peer into the room.

Tommy's sitting at the table, a nice full plate in front of him. Dad and Mum are sitting in front of their plates, too, but no-one is eating.

How is it?

I lick my lips and glance at my bowl, which is bright and shining. I've already eaten up my supper, but I wouldn't mind getting a bit more... if they're not hungry perhaps they could give me some of their food?

I tilt my head to better consider how many chances I might have of this really happening, then I see Corrado stand up and go to Tommy. There's a nasty expression on his face.

I start grumbling again. There's something wrong in the air tonight.

Tommy's keeping his eyes on his plate and he's poking at the food with a fork.

"You must tell the truth!" Corrado bursts out in a

threatening voice. "Remember you have nothing to gain from silence."

Oh, bother! I can see Corrado is fuming with rage. It isn't wise to stay near him when he's in one of his moods. I start barking and I mean to say: "Go, Tommy go! Run away as fast as you can!" But Tommy doesn't even turn his head. It looks as if he couldn't hear me!

"So? Haven't you got anything to tell me?" Corrado asks. The words sound like stones he's throwing against Tommy's face.

I bark again. "Run Tommy, run! Run and hide somewhere before it's too late!"

But Tommy doesn't take notice of me at all, no matter how hard I try. I decide that just barking is not enough, so I add bouncing and whining. But Tommy keeps staring at the food on his plate.

"I want you to tell the truth!" Corrado yells. "So? I think I asked you a question!"

"I told the truth!" Tommy screams.

Oh, no, no, no, no!!! What a mistake! One must never, NEVER ANSWER BACK!!!

I'm so frustrated that I can't help going back to the olive tree. I run around it a couple of times then I go back to the window.

Corrado has drawn a chair next to Tommy now and he is talking to him. His voice is so low that I can hear only a few of the words he says: "it was you... changing rooms... every time ... things .... stealing from bags... cellphone... money... video-game..."

"I didn't do that!"

Oh, no, Tommy's answered back again! Now I don't know what Corrado will do to him!

And I can't do anything to help him!

What can I do? Isn't there ANYTHING I CAN DO?

I go back to the olive tree and I run around it over and over again.

I sometimes run around bushes and trees. There's a deep furrow around the olive tree and there's another one around the jasmine bush, and another around the cherry tree. The grass doesn't grow in these furrows any longer and Corrado and Marianna get mad at me for making them. But there's nothing I can do about this. There are moments when I absolutely need to run around a tree, I don't know why.

So I keep running until I suddenly remember that Tommy is in danger and I run back to the window.

Corrado is still talking to him, but now his voice is loud enough and I can hear all the words he's saying... "...our wallets. We thought we were imagining things at first, but we no longer think so now. I recently found one hundred Euros had disappeared from my wallet."

"I didn't take your money!" Tommy shouts.

"I'm not so sure!" Corrado shouts back. "I also thought you liked playing soccer, or so you made me think, but the coach said that you don't work hard enough, that you like sitting on the bench... and last Saturday you locked yourself in the changing rooms during the match. Did you do this to be sure no-one could find you out while you were stealing?"

Tommy suddenly stands up and throws his fork away. It lands on the floor with a clang that makes me startle and sends Marianna up yelling: "Pick it up immediately!"

"No!" Tommy screams and sits down again bursting into loud sobs, his head in his hands.

My heart sinks.

"Pick it up!" Corrado yells. "Do it now." His face is purple red and it looks as if his eyes were going to pop out of his head.

"I didn't take the money!" Tommy screams

"If you didn't, explain to me why..." Corrado starts, but Tommy stands up and shouts: "I hate you!"

WHAT DID HE SAY?

"What did you say?" Corrado yells.

"I hate you!" Tommy shouts again "I hate you both!"

A resounding slap lands on Tommy's face.

Tommy's eyes open wide and I throw myself against the window foaming with rage.

"Calm down!" Marianna says. She's now standing between Tommy and Corrado.

Tommy finally does what he should have done from the very beginning. He runs away. I can hear the thudding of his shoes up the stairs.

Marianna follows him.

Corrado is alone now. He keeps standing for a while, his head lowered, then he sits down at the table and starts eating.

Then Marianna comes back. "He locked himself in." she says "Anyway, we talked through the door and he promised he'll speak to the coach tomorrow."

Corrado shrugs and goes on eating.

I go back to the olive tree and I start running again. It takes a long time before I can make myself stop.

When I finally do, I sit on the grass and I peer at the moon.

Tonight it's not so big and round as it was yesterday, but the patches on its skin are so clear that perhaps I'll be able to see if it's hairy all over like me.

I peer and peer, but can't see any hairs.

CHAPTER SEVEN

(Wednesday, 20th July)

The Trap

I catch the ball and dribble down the field, then I pass it to Viani, who kicks it back to me. Two opponents are tackling me now, Martini is one of them. He lunges for the ball and brushes me aside. This is the right time for me to take the chance, I decide, and I topple over as if I'd been badly shoved. I remain face down on the ground.

The coach whistles and stops the game.

Martini is now gawking at me from above. "Don't be a dummy, Aladino, I didn't even touch you!" he spouts.

I squeeze my eyes and I do as if I want to sit up, then I grimace and flop down again. "Ouch!" I mumble, making my voice hoarse and bending my left arm against my chest.

Beppe comes to me carrying the first-aid kit. "What are you trying to do Tommaso Aladino? Everybody saw that you did it all by yourself."

 "Ouch!" I cry again. "It's my arm... It hurts..."

"Can you stand on your legs?"

I nod, then I shake my head. "I don't know." I reply in a strained voice.

"Let's get out of here, so the others can go on playing." Beppe says.

I let Beppe help me stand up and then I stumble

toward the bench holding my arm up against my chest.

The coach glances at me grimly. "In trouble again?" he sputters.

"I hurt myself." I grumble, sitting down.

Beppe leans over me. "Hold your arm up so that I can see it." he orders.

"I can't." I say in a plaintive voice.

Beppe takes my arm and gently tries to stretch it, but I cry out in pain.

"Show me where it hurts." he says.

I think I've finally convinced him as he sounds more concerned now. "All over here." I say, vaguely pointing at my forearm.

"Here?" asks Beppe touching my wrist. Then he starts moving it gently.

"Ouch!"

"Funny it hurts so much. Did you fall onto your hand?"

I nod.

"There's no swelling though and no loss of movement. It doesn't look like a sprain or a fracture." Beppe says, pensively scratching his nose with his forefinger. "Well, let's see what we can do."

He takes a small can out of the first-aid kit and sprays my arm. Then he wraps my wrist in a stretchy bandage. Finally, he binds a scarf behind my head and orders: "Put your arm inside here and keep it there. Does it still hurt badly? If it does we'll have to take you to the doctor at once. The sooner the better."

"I feel much better now!" I exclaim. I wouldn't want them to take me to a doctor! That would spoil my plans and a doctor would immediately see there's nothing wrong with my wrist.

"OK, then. Let's see how you feel in half an hour's time. Just sit here and don't move."

"Fine." I say.

I sit on the bench and keep glancing at the coach to

see if he's paying any attention to me, but he keeps shouting and yelling to the other players and he doesn't seem to know I'm here.

Now that I'm in the middle of it all I feel so tense! One of the reasons is that I haven't seen The Two yet and I fear they may not be here today. Then I say to myself I needn't worry about this as they won't certainly want to miss the fifty Euros I have to give them, but a pang of anxiety grips me all the same. The fact is I didn't have enough time to plan everything carefully, as the idea came to me all of a sudden.

It all started while Dad was driving me to the bus stop. I didn't say a word to him because I was still furious. I couldn't forgive him for slapping me and for all the things he'd said to me. I was so mad at him! I was mad at the coach, too. I couldn't believe he thought I LIKED SITTING ON THE BENCH! Really!!!

It was Dad who suddenly started talking.

"Don't tell the coach." he said.

I glanced at him in surprise. I couldn't believe he'd started to talk to me! But I was not going to relent, I decided, so I kept my mouth shut.

"I mean... You'd better not tell the coach what I told... um... what I told you last night. You see... I ... I promised I wouldn't tell you." Dad stuttered.

Blimey! Was Dad FEELING ASHAMED or what?

"So, you won't tell the coach, will you?" Dad asked again.

I shook my head and started thinking. Was it good or bad that the coach didn't know I knew?

It might be good, I decided, as that might give me the chance to try and solve my problem somehow.

But at first I didn't know how to do it. What I knew for sure, though, was that the coach wouldn't believe me if I told him I'd never stolen anything! He'd already decided I was a thief and that was the end of it.

And what if I told him about The Two?

I immediately decided that wasn't a good idea for two reasons: the first was that he would probably think I was only trying to get away with it, the second was that if The Two found out I'd spied on them they'd make me pay for it.

I kept racking my brain till I got to the soccer field but the very idea the coach would be talking to me soon scared me so much that I couldn't think clearly.

Then, when I saw that he didn't seem to be interested in talking to me, I thought he was probably taking his time to see if he could catch me stealing in the changing rooms, and that gave me the idea. What if he caught The Two there instead? That would put an end to the problem, wouldn't it? But what could I possibly do to make this happen?

In the end, I decided that the best thing to do was to behave in the same way as I had always done. So I would have to pretend that I wasn't feeling well and that I needed to go to the changing rooms. Perhaps the coach would come after me thinking he'd catch me red handed. But he'd have to find The Two in the changing rooms, not me!

When I first made this plan I felt sure it would work, but now I'm so scared! The only thing that cheers me up a bit is the spell.

Because I did cast the spell after all!

I'm now wearing inside-out underpants and two pairs of socks on each foot, with the odd ones hidden below so that nobody can see them. And this morning I got up at dawn, went to the lawn, merged my fingers in the wet grass, touched my forehead with it, put some salt on the tip of my tongue... it had to be table salt as I couldn't find the other kind. I also sat on the floor and drew an imaginary circle all around myself using a twig I'd picked up in the garden. Then I recited all those stupid verses over and over again, not just ten, but a hundred times, I think.

"How's your wrist? Wouldn't you by any chance like to go to the changing rooms for a while and have a nice little rest?"

I startle and look up at the coach. His gentle manner and honeyed tones reassure me. He seems to be thinking he's setting a trap for me. I hope he doesn't realize it's me who's setting a trap for him.

"May I?" I ask looking up at him with innocent eyes.

"Yes, on you go!" the coach says, a big grin on his face.

"Thanks a lot." I mutter, standing up.

Everything seems to be getting on well so far. I can go on with my plan then. I only have to keep my head strong and not panic.

"Don't you need the key?"

"Oh, yes, I guess. Thanks."

I take the key from his hands and I immediately head

towards the changing rooms playing the role of the suffering hero. So I walk away slowly, limping a bit and keeping my head lowered, all the while praying: "Look at me! Look at me now!"

I'd really like to turn round just to check if the coach is looking at me, but I can't do that, of course. That would spoil everything!

But as soon as I get out of the field and start walking along the lane that leads to the changing rooms, I decide the right moment has come to set up the main scene. So I pull the scarf away from my neck, thrust it into my pocket and break into a run, keeping my head up and moving my arms evenly to show there has never been any injury at all.

I only hope the coach has not lost interest and is still keeping his eyes on me!

LOOK AT ME, PLEASE, LOOK AT ME! I repeat to myself while I'm running.

If the coach is still looking at me he'll realize his

suspicions were right and he'll follow me into the changing rooms as soon as he thinks it safe.

I keep running and I only slow down when I get into the thicket. I'm sure he can no longer see me here. My only wish now is that The Two are inside.

I stop dead. I hadn't thought of that! How stupid of me!

HOW SO VERY STUPID!

If The Two are inside they'll most probably catch sight of me as soon as I get out of the thicket!

WHAT CAN I DO?

The only other solution would be hiding somewhere, but where could I hide?

As I'm trying to think of a way to get out of this mess, I head back towards the soccer field, but as I get to the edge of the thicket I catch sight of the coach coming over.

That's exactly what I wanted him to do, but now I have to hide from him, too!

How stupid of me not thinking about that before!

I NEED TO HIDE SOMEWHERE!

I look frenziedly around but I can't see any hiding places. This ridiculous thicket of scanty trees is good to hide someone from afar but not at a close distance. I run back to the edge of the thicket and I see that the coach is already quite near.

THERE'S NO TIME LEFT! I MUST VANISH!

Or perhaps I'd better go to the changing rooms, after all! If The Two see me coming they'll stay put to get the money.

But if the coach finds all of us in there he'll certainly think we are accomplices and this will make things worse!

But what if THE TWO SEE THE COACH?

They'll run away, won't they?

HOW STUPID OF ME!

Why didn't I think of this before?

What if I wait for the coach and talk to him here on the

spot? If he believes what I say, we might go to the changing rooms together.

But what if THE TWO AREN'T THERE?

And if THEY ARE?

If they are there and they see me coming along with the coach they'll think I've spied on them and this will make things worse.

MUCH WORSE!

I have no choice.

I MUST DISAPPEAR.

Vanished!

There's

a deep silence in the garden today.

It sounds as if the wind was keeping its breath.

Even the flies have stopped buzzing and all the birds seem to have vanished. No twittering from the tree branches, no flapping of wings. Also the butterflies seem to have hidden in some secret place of their own. Even the sun is still. It usually moves about sending small spots of light to waver in the breeze, but today the spots are all stuck in their places. Also the flowers keep as still as possible. Perhaps they know the slightest movement might make them tumble down from their stalks.

A sudden thud next to my nose gives me a startle. It

was only a poor pomegranate flower falling down onto the grass. I sniff the desolate flower for a while, then I yawn and tell myself that even time doesn't seem to be moving today.

Such a long wait!

I wonder what I'm waiting for...

Ah, yes, I remember now! I'm waiting for Tommy, of course! He's generally back when the sun is high in the sky. Now the sun is already quite low, but Tommy isn't back yet.

This morning he appeared when it was still dark, he touched the grass, then he touched his brow, then he picked up a twig from the ground, then he patted me on the head, then he went back in without saying a word. Such strange things for him to do!

I stand up and move along a bit to get into the shadow, I turn round a couple of times and I lie down again. I sigh. I close my eyes...

Is this Tommy's voice I'm hearing? Is he back at last? I open my eyes and jump up.

There's a group of people in the garden, but Tommy doesn't seem to be among them. What's up?

I see Marianna come towards me. Her eyes are swollen, she has a very white face and her hair's a mess. She's clutching a hanky and she's shaking all over.

What happened?

Then Corrado arrives, wearing his usual grim look.

After him come two more people. Who are they? I've never seen them before.

I move backward and start sniffing.

"Is this the dog?" one of the two blokes asks. He bends down and keeps his fingers joined together as if he was holding some food in them. "Come on, old boy, come and see what I've got in here!" he says.

Does he think I'm stupid? Does he really think I believe he's got some food in his hand? I move back and start growling.

"Let me do it." Corrado says, moving forward.

Before I have the time to think, Corrado grabs my collar and puts me on the leash. "Smell this!" he orders, shoving a piece of clothing under my nose.

I smell as I am told, but there's no need for me to do that, really! I already know this is Tommy's t-shirt, no doubt. And now that I have smelled it, what should I do?

"Come on, Teodorico. Come with us. We'll have to go and look for Tommy."

Teodorico? How strange! He's never called me by my first name before. And what did he say? Look for Tommy? Why? Where's Tommy? I think back to the mountain, when he almost got lost. Has this happened again? I feel hairs rise on my back. How can I find him if I have no idea where he is?

"Come on, let's go!"

I move on with the group.

Corrado makes me jump into the boot, then he sits at the wheel. Marianna sits next to him. Both bang the doors shut and Corrado pulls out. The tires squeal as we speed out of the gate, following the other car with the two blokes.

What's going on? Where are they taking me?

Why aren't they saying a word?

I stand up and look at the road.

Suddenly Marianna starts sobbing.

Corrado gives a quick glance at her but he doesn't say a word.

"Where can he have gone?" Marianna stutters between sobs.

"The dog will find him now, you'll see."

I prick up my ears.

"And what if he's been kidnapped..."

Corrado snorts. "That's nonsense, really! Why should he have been kidnapped? You know what I think? I think he must have got on the wrong bus and he may be coming back home right now."

Marianna screams: "How can you say that? Don't you know there's only one bus at that terminal? And the bus driver says no-one got on the bus at the terminal today."

Corrado answers in a low, tense voice. "This is why we're taking the dog there! Just to see if he can find out which direction he may have taken."

Marianna breaks into another outburst of sobs.

I lick my lips and I wonder. What did Corrado say I should do?

We are now going uphill along a winding road. This reminds me of the mountain and I can't help smiling a bit.

"Where's he? Where's he gone?" Marianna's voice startles me out of my happy thoughts.

"He may have walked down the hill." Corrado says.

"Why should he have done that?"

Corrado shrugs. "Who knows?" he says.

"Don't you realize it's seven thirty already?   If he'd
walked down the hill he should have been home by now!
Don't you realize it will soon be dark? What if we don't find
him before it gets dark?"

"It won't be dark until after half past eight. We still have
plenty of time."

Marianna bursts into sobs again. Then she stops and
cries: "It's all your fault! You shouldn't have turned on him
as you did last night!"

Corrado sighs audibly but keeps silent.

 "It's all your fault!" she cries out again. "And the
coach's fault! Both of you turning on him like that! And
he was clean, the poor boy! It was those two thugs that
did all the stealing! And the coach never found out until
today! Don't you realize they'd been wandering about and
mixing with the boys for days? And the coach had never
bothered! And he put all the blame on our innocent son!
And they even had marijuana on them? The rascals! And

they were left free to wander around… and you even slapped poor Tommy last night!"

"Stop it now, for God's sake!" Corrado shouts. "I've had more than enough of your accusations!"

Marianna drops silent and Corrado drives on without saying one more word. After a while he stops the car and I jump out of the boot. Then we start walking up a grassy slope. Corrado is now keeping me on such a short leash that I risk treading his shoes at every step we take.

A square bloke, looking like a wardrobe, comes towards us. "Nothing yet." he says, scratching his shiny, bald head.

A group of boys, looking more or less like Tommy, comes towards me.

"What a nice dog! It's quite big, isn't it?" says one of them.

"I didn't know Tommy Aladino had a dog!" says another.

"He's got such a comic face!" says one more.

"He looks smart. I like him." says the first.

I wag my tail. I'd love to have a good chat with these kids but Marianna kneels at my side and starts patting my head. "Go, Teodorico, there's a good boy... find Tommy, will you?" she pleads. I see she's still crying.

Corrado comes and shoves Tommy's shirt under my nose again. He orders: "Go for Tommy. Find him!"

I thrust my nose into the grass and start wandering about, pulling Corrado after me.

There are all sorts of different scents here.

It takes me some time but I finally land on a faint trace. This is Tommy's odour, I'm sure. I move forward, following it, then backwards, then I circle around, then I move forward again and I finally end up where I started.

"Perhaps we'd better take him towards the changing rooms." suggests the wardrobe man. Corrado nods and pulls me on until we get to a dirty lane which winds away from the field and leads to a thicket of small trees.

The lane is bordered by a line of cypresses on one side and by a thick, tall hedge on the other.

"I last saw him run along this alley on his way to the changing rooms." says the wardrobe man.

I start sniffing and moving around, my nose level with the ground. Then I briskly stop. There's such a nice smell of frogs here! It reminds me of the mountain so much that I can't help lingering about a little bit.

Corrado leans down to inspect the spot of ground I'm sniffing as if he expected to see Tommy jump out of it at any moment. Then, when he realizes I'm wasting my time, he pulls himself up and orders: "Come on, Teodorico, get going."

I sigh and start moving towards the trees. When I get into the thicket I find a slight trace of Tommy's scent again. I follow it, pulling Corrado behind me. If I only could run about freely and go wherever I want and not have to drag Corrado like this! I'm so tired and thirsty! And I've started panting hard and coughing. My throat is so dry it hurts. Another problem is that there are too many different scents all around and it's not easy to stick to Tommy's odour for very long.

But then I finally find the scent again. It's stronger than the one I'd found in the field but, again, it goes up and down, up and down, and up and down again. I pull Corrado forward and backward a number of times and then I finally head for the thick hedge on one side of the alley.

Tommy's odour is very strong here and there's a small opening at the foot of the hedge. I sniff at it accurately and I understand that Tommy must have thrust himself into the hedge somehow. I pull as hard as I can until Corrado lets go of the leash and I get into the hole. Tommy has been here!

"He can't have got inside there. This hedge is far too thick!" I hear the wardrobe man say, but I know he's wrong! I know for sure Tommy has been here.

The sharp ends of broken twigs scratch me all over but they won't stop me now that Tommy's smell is so strong, so I force my way through the vegetation until I get to the other side of the hedge and I suddenly find myself on the brink of a chasm and before I know what's happening, I start skidding down a steep slope overgrown with weeds. I try to stop, but I simply can't. My legs keep going and I have to run full speed to try and keep my balance. But then I stumble against a rock and right at the same time the leash gets trapped.

For a long moment I hang from the leash, my legs helplessly dangling in the air and my collar chocking me. Then whatever was holding the leash breaks and I tumble down the slope. I roll down, and roll and roll, the sky and the ground alternating in quick succession until I finally bump against the trunk of a fallen tree and stop.

I close my eyes trying to understand if I'm still whole,

then I suddenly smell Tommy's scent. It's so strong and so near! I start sniffing the nettles, the brambles and the rotting wood spasmodically and I finally see him! He's lying still, his head turned to the side.

I 'd like to start bouncing for joy but I suddenly feel a horrible, stabbing pain in one of my fore legs.

I whine at the top of my voice and then I sit down to lick my leg. What a horrible pain! I must have also been stung by nettles as I'm itching and burning all over. I look up at the hedge which hems the slope, far away over my head. Then I peer at Tommy again.

Why isn't he moving? His face is half hidden by the nettles. His legs are badly scratched and covered in blood.

Oh, dear me, what happened to him? I send a howl into the air and then I start licking Tommy's hair and face. I also poke at his chest with my good paw, but he doesn't stir.

I go back to howling, my face up to the sky.

Then I turn to look at Tommy again. This time I catch sight of a flicker of his eyelids and I go back to licking him until he finally pulls himself up and squints at me. "What happened?" he mutters.

I don't know, but we must get away from here! The shadows are getting longer and it will be dark soon. I bark and howl to make Tommy understand what I mean and then I stop because I hear a noise.

What is it? It's coming from the hedge up the slope. It's just like the buzzing noise of the lawn-mower. Only much louder.

I look up and I see there are some people looking down. I can also hear their voices. "He's there!" He's there, look!" "They're both down there!" And Marianna's voice among the others: "Where are they? I can't see them! Let me see them!"

I howl to the sky in an outburst of joy, then I flatten down next to Tommy and go back to whining and whimpering and licking my leg.

When I look up again I see there's a bloke hanging on to the end of a rope.

Tommy looks up, too. "They're coming for us." he says. Then he places his hand on my head and murmurs: "Thank you so much Teo. You saved my life."

CHAPTER EIGHT

(Thursday, 21st July)

Telling the Truth

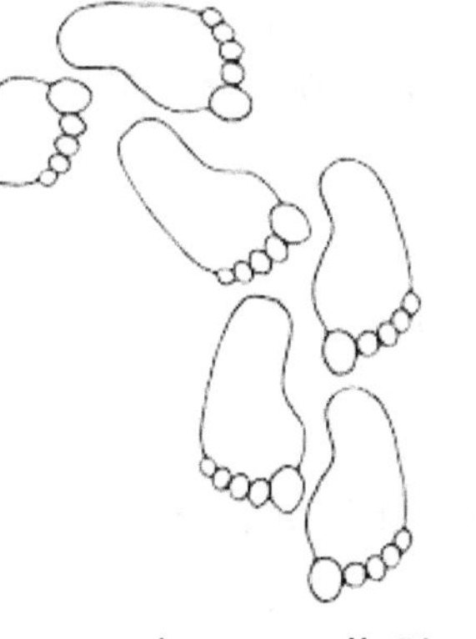

It's

ten fifty-five and eleven seconds...

I haven't made up my mind on what I'm going to tell Giselle yet. The fact is, I don't want to make a fool of myself.

What did I have in mind that day? I really don't know. I saw it there among the others, "NEW" printed in glittering block letters on the jacket and that beautiful picture of the medieval castle... the armours... the prince... the princess...

the jester...

I liked it because the characters looked really horrified so I thought it might be about ghosts or zombies... I adore horror films, and a horror video-game promised to be even better than a film...

I later found out it was only rats. If I'd known, I wouldn't have stolen the video, I think. I don't mean to say I don't get a bit squeamish when I see rats, but they're not so very scary, only disgusting...

Anyway, that day I badly wanted a new game. I hadn't bought one for ages. The last one had been *The Frogs*, which I had to pay for with two washing ups and ten table settings... and after that, I realized it hadn't been worth the effort as at school everyone kept saying: "Ah, that game! I know it! How boring! It's an old one..." and things like that.

What time is it now? Still seventeen minutes and fifty seconds to go. I can stay in bed for another ten minutes. I must keep an eye on the clock though, I don't want to be late. I want to get away with this other problem once and for all.

Giselle came to the fence this morning and she spotted me as I was standing by the gate. I pretended not to see her, but she cried out at me: "What happened? Did you have an accident?"

"Not at all!" I said, not budging an inch in the hope she didn't notice the bruises on my face.

"What are those bruises and scratches on your face then?"

I shrugged. "Oh, nothing." I said. "See you later."

"What happened to Teodorico's leg? Is it in plaster?" she went on mercilessly as she saw Teo limp to her on three legs.

"Oh, it's nothing serious!"

"Why was there such a huge crowd in your garden last night?" she went on implacably, and I realized there was nothing to do. I would have to talk to her sooner or later.

"Later! I shouted "I'll tell you later."

"When?"

"I can't right now." I insisted.

"What about meeting at the Den?"

I was so shocked at hearing her talk about the Den so openly and in such a loud voice I hurried towards her before she gave our secret away. "Don't shout like that!" I hissed when I was near the fence. "Someone might hear you!"

"OK. So, what about meeting at the Den?" she said very quietly, gawking at my face.

"When?"

"Tonight."

"What time?"

"Eleven fifteen?"

"Fine."

That was settled for the moment and I felt a little relieved, but now I wish I hadn't made any promise. I don't really know what I'll be telling her!

What time is it? Two minutes to eleven already. I'd better wake Teo up. He's fast asleep, poor chap, he won't like the idea of getting out at this time of the night, but I don't feel like going on my own.

Who would have ever imagined? Teo can sleep in my bedroom now! He's become a hero and his only other name is Teodorico, no longer just the dog, silly dog or stupid beast. And Mum keeps giving him biscuits. He'll become a tub of lard if he goes on eating like that!

Mum also bought him this huge fluffy cushion so that he'd not be tempted to jump onto my bed, she said. Poor Teo! Fancy him jumping around with his leg in a cast!

What is really amazing, though, is that I only got bruises and scratches. I could have broken my neck, they said at the hospital. But I was sent back home almost at once while poor Teo broke his leg and had to spend the whole night at the vet.

I hadn't realized there was a precipice. I was trying to hide from the coach and I thrust myself into the vegetation until I suddenly was on the other side of the hedge. I was in such a fluster that I just stepped on among the tall weeds growing all over the place without realizing there was that huge gap and before I knew what was happening I was rolling down the slope and vainly trying to grab at something that might stop my fall, until I eventually bumped into something hard. After that, I must have fainted because the next thing I remember is Teo licking my face.

If he had not come for me I would probably still be lying there. He was so clever finding me down there! Who else would have thought of that hole? I think it's only fair to say that Teo saved my life. I'm so sorry he broke his leg, though, poor chap! Luckily, the vet said he'll make a full recovery.

And as for me, I'm so glad I've got rid of the problem!

Unfortunately, I had to own up to stealing the video-game, so we'll have to go back to the shop, apologize and pay the money back.

Giving back all the money I stole will eat up my future pocket money for ages and I don't want to think of all the chores I'll have to do for the rest of the summer! I bet I'll be glad to go back to school when the time comes.

 It will be much worse for The Two, though. I know they have been arrested and charged with illegal detention of drugs, stealing and physical assault.

It's lucky they didn't get away with it! Apparently, when they saw the coach coming and tried to run away, they both slipped on the wet floor and tumbled down, one on top of the other. So the coach found them in a heap, all the stolen things still in their pockets. The funny thing, though, is that no-one could explain how the floor could have been so thoroughly flooded with soapy water, the more so that there were no leaks from the taps or the showers!

As for me, I was a real fool, I admit. I didn't think twice about it as there was such a huge crowd of boy-scouts in the shop, all of them flitting around the shelves and picking up all sorts of things, the shop-owner doing nothing to stop them.

So I slipped the video-game under my jacket and headed for the door but, as soon as I put my foot out of the shop, The Two cornered me against the wall.

"Look at this smelly sack of rat guts. Where do you think you're going?" one of them said, coming so close to me that we stood nose to nose.

"Where do you think you're going, you nitwit? We saw what you did!" said the other, poking at my chest with his forefinger.

"Now we're going to call the police!" the first threatened.

"Good idea!" the other said.

"No, don't please!" I pleaded "I'll put it back straight away!"

"Put it back? Ha, Ha! Listen to the idiot! He thinks he can put it back! Ha! Ha!" sneered the first.

"Think of the owner's face when the nitwit puts the game back!" laughed the other.

"Please, take the video" I said, pulling it out from under my jacket, "but don't tell the owner please."

"Oh, really! Just listen to him! What have you got in your stupid head? Do you think you can sell this to us?" said the first, his red eyes popping out of his head.

"You know what? We're going to sell it to you and you can keep it." said the other.

"That's settled! It's a bargain we're offering. Give us 20 Euros and we're even!" said the first.

"I have no money on me." I muttered.

"No problem. We know where we can find you. Just

take the money with you next time you come to the football ground." said the first, poking at my chest with his finger again.

"OK." I said, chocking back the tears.

Right then the whole group of scouts swarmed out of the shop and I managed to mix with them. Luckily, the bus was coming right at that moment and I slipped in as soon as the doors opened. I went to sit at the back and I tried to see if the The Two were still in sight, but they seemed to have disappeared.

It took me the whole trip to fight back the tears and I even thought of leaving the video-game on the bus seat. Then I realized this would not solve the problem and I put it inside my bag instead.

What time is it? Two minutes past eleven.

In three minutes sharp I'll wake Teo up. I'm afraid he'll make a lot of noise coming downstairs on three legs. Anyway, he would never forgive me if I left him here all alone. He might even start howling and Mum and Dad would come running to see what happened. If they don't find me in my bed they'll get a heart attack, after all that happened.

Mum keeps saying she thought she was going to die on the spot when she realized I wasn't on the bus and right at the same time the coach called her cell-phone asking if I had got home safe and sound!

"What do you mean? Tommy was not on the bus! I was just going to call you! He must still be there!" Mum had screamed.

"He's not here! He must have gone away before time, as he sometimes does. But the funny thing is that he's left his bag in the changing rooms!" the coach had screamed back.

Mum now swears she doesn't know how she could have survived all that. Poor mum! I gave her such a fright!

What time is it? It's eleven, four minutes and three

seconds. Time to wake up Teo and go.

The Scent of the Night

W_{hat} is it? Who's pulling at my collar? Is it Tommy?

Yes, it's him! But it can't be morning yet! It's too dark! I'm so sleepy and I was having such a funny dream...

I close my eyes and try to get back to the dream. It was about Bigongio... Bigongio who could no longer climb up the same old tree... how amazing!

... I've even stopped barking!

What's the sense of pretending
I'm chasing him?
I sit on the grass
and I patiently wait for him
to get to the top of the tree.
But he just can't!
Poor Bigongio,
he's become too fat!
He gets midway up
then he rolls down again.
I look away.
I don't want him to think
that I'm staring...

Oh, bother, who's pulling at my collar?

"Wake up, Teo!"

I yawn and open one eye. Tommy is hovering over me.
His feet are near my head, shoes and all.

"Get up, I said!"

I yawn again, then I sit up painfully. This leg is a real nuisance.

"Don't make any noise." Tommy whispers as we get down the stairs.

As if that was easy, having to walk on three legs!

Tommy is wearing a light on his forehead and as soon as we are out he rushes down the lawn. He's going to the Den, of course.

I follow him as fast as I can but when I get to the tunnel he's already disappeared down the hole. My tail sags. He could have waited for me! Doesn't he know I can't bend my leg?

I duck my head and put my tail between my legs, but I'm still too tall for the tunnel, so my back gets brushed by the leaves and stung by the thorns as I go.

Before I get there, I hear Giselle say: "Now tell me what happened." and as I sit down next to them at last, Tommy says: " It's a long story..."

"I love long stories." Giselle says.

Humph! If it's a long story I might as well go back to sleep. I yawn, I turn round a couple of times to make my bed and I lie down.

"OK... well... you see..." Tommy says, clearing his voice, "these three nerds... big blokes, you know... punks"

"Punks?"

"You know... those guys who wear spiky crests on their heads..."

"OK, I got it, so?"

"So, as I was saying... these punks, you know, with piercings all over..."

"Piercings?"

"Yes, those rings or studs you pierce your skin with and wear on your ears, nose, eyebrows... even on your tongue sometimes... got it?"

"Yuck! Doesn't it hurt?"

"I'm sure it does."

"So why do they do that?"

"No idea."

"I see. So, you were telling me about these punks..."

"They had started bullying a friend of mine... a real chicken, you know...."

"A chicken?"

"Yes, a shy, weak, rather short bloke..."

"What's his name?"

"Er... Marco."

"And what did those thugs do to this... Marco?"

"They bullied him... pestered him for money..."

"Why?"

"Well, you know, because this bloke, I mean, this Marco, as I said, did not have the courage to fight back..."

"Couldn't he have told someone?"

"Well, actually, he told me!"

"Did he?"

"Yes."

"And what did you do?"

"I fought against the thugs."

"Did you? Weren't you scared?"

"Well, you know, I cast the spell."

There's a brief silence. Then Giselle says: "Really? I can't believe it!"

"I did. I decided to give it a try."

"And did it work?" Giselle asks eagerly.

"It did."

"And what happened?"

"Well, as I was saying, I cast the spell... I put odd socks on and all the rest... and then I went to the football ground..."

"So it all happened at the football ground!"

"Yes, didn't I say that before?"

"You didn't. So... that's why you couldn't play... I mean...

you had problems... perhaps you were worried about your friend, I mean..."

"Kind of. So, as I was saying... these two thugs..."

"You said three!"

"Yes, well, but one didn't turn up."

"I see..."

"So, these two thugs... I caught them beating my friend, you know, and I fought against them. I gave one of them a punch on the nose, then grabbed the other with my left hand, made my secret karate chop and grounded him. Then, when the other came over I..."

"OK, I get it. And what happened after that?"

"So Marco ran away and fell into a sort of crevice."

"Marco?"

"Yea."

"And what about you?"

"I ran after him and fell into the crevice too. Luckily Teo found me... I mean us, so we were rescued... but Teo broke his leg, unfortunately, so…"

I suddenly feel the touch of Giselle's hand on my head. It's so soothing! "Poor Teo… you were so brave!" she says. Then she kisses me on the nose and I feel all my pains melt away. Before I can even realize it, I start singing…

What a heaaaaavenly bliiiiisss …
What a wooooooonderful kiiiiisss …
What a beauuuuutiiiiiiiful niiiiiight…
This is loooooooove at first siiiiiight…

"Poor Teo, just listen to him howling so sadly! He must be in such pain!" Giselle says.

"Yes, poor old thing. He saved my life, you know…"

"I know… but you didn't tell me the whole story, did you? " Giselle says.

There's a sudden silence and I close my eyes. I rack my brain trying to bring this other bloke, Marco, back to my mind, but I can't seem to be able to. I must have forgotten him.

Now Tommy and Giselle have started talking again, but I'm not listening any more. I'm too sleepy....

"Wake up Teo! We're going back to bed."

Good gosh! What is it now? I was dreaming about Bigongio again. He'd got down the tree and he was scowling at me with his disquieting yellow eyes. Why was he scowling at me? Why wasn't he running away? Wasn't he scared of me?

"Come on, Teo! We've got to go." Tommy says.

 I pull myself up and I scratch my ear. I see that Giselle is going away right now. I take a big sigh and I walk behind Tommy, the thorns scratching my back again, but at last we are out.

What a beautiful night! All so calm... all so quiet...

to tell the truth, I'd rather stay here than go back inside.

If I had my cushion with me...

I could sleep on the lawn
and sing to the moon
and dream my own dreams
until it is dawn...
dreams about Bigongio,
and about buried bones,
and about chasing rabbits,
grasshoppers and frogs,
squirrels and hares,
rats and hedgehogs...
and I could smell the heavenly
scent of the night:
the perfume of flowers,
the moss on old wood,
the soggy toadstools,
the droppings of bats,
the pee-pee of cats...

"What are you doing Teo? Why aren't you coming?"

"Can't you hear me, Teo?

...

Come on! Can't you hear me?"

...

"Teo!!! What's the matter? Why aren't you coming?

...

If you don't come at once I'll leave you there! I mean it!!!"

The End

Finito di stampare nel mese di Dicembre 2015
per conto di Youcanprint *Self-Publishing*